# DANGEROUS KISS

A BILLIONAIRE ROMANCE

MICHELLE LOVE

HOT AND STEAMY ROMANCE

# CONTENTS

*About the Author*   vii
*Blurb*   ix

1. Chapter One — 1
2. Chapter Two — 11
3. Chapter Three — 18
4. Chapter Four — 26
5. Chapter Five — 32
6. Chapter Six — 41
7. Chapter Seven — 47
8. Chapter Eight — 58
9. Chapter Nine — 64
10. Chapter Ten — 71
11. Chapter Eleven — 73
12. Chapter Twelve — 79
13. Chapter Thirteen — 88
14. Chapter Fourteen — 94
15. Chapter Fifteen — 100
16. Chapter Sixteen — 107
17. Chapter Seventeen — 112
18. Chapter Eighteen — 115
19. Chapter Nineteen — 121
20. Chapter Twenty — 125
21. Chapter Twenty-One — 132
22. Chapter Twenty-Two — 135
23. Chapter Twenty-Three — 141
24. Chapter Twenty-Four — 145
25. Chapter Twenty-Five — 149
26. Chapter Twenty-Six — 154
27. Chapter Twenty-Seven — 156

    Sign Up to Receive Free Books — 165
    Preview of Dark Masquerade — 166

28. Venice, Italy — 168

| | |
|---|---|
| *Other Books By This Author* | 235 |
| *About the Author* | 237 |
| *Copyright* | 239 |

Made in "The United States" by:

Michelle Love

© Copyright 2020 – Michelle Love

ISBN: 978-1-64808-064-7

**ALL RIGHTS RESERVED.** No part of this publication may be reproduced or transmitted in any form whatsoever, electronic, or mechanical, including photocopying, recording, or by any informational storage or retrieval system without express written, dated and signed permission from the author

❦ Created with Vellum

## ABOUT THE AUTHOR

Mrs. Love writes about smart, sexy women and the hot alpha billionaires who love them. She has found her own happily ever after with her dream husband and adorable 6 and 2 year old kids.

Currently, Michelle is hard at work on the next book in the series, and trying to stay off the Internet.

"Thank you for supporting an indie author. Anything you can do, whether it be writing a review, or even simply telling a fellow reader that you enjoyed this. Thanks

# BLURB

Movie director Cosimo DeLuca may be at the top of his game but on his latest shoot, he is already regretting hiring diva Stella Reckless as his leading lady. Fending off her advances, the recently widowed Cosimo had no intention of ever falling in love again—until he meets Stella's long-suffering personal assistant, Biba May. Their attraction becomes red-hot, and soon they begin to discover a whole new world of erotic pleasure. Biba is the only one who can handle Stella, and although the actress treats Biba appallingly, she would be lost without her. When she sees the obvious love between Cosimo and Biba, her bitchiness makes Biba's life a misery. Throw in a mysterious stalker, determined to get close to Stella, and Biba soon finds herself in a troubling situation.
But when Stella's stalker shifts his focus to Biba, a dangerous game unfolds which could cost Biba more than her job.
Can Cosimo give her the lifeline she needs, or will Biba be pulled into a mire of betrayal and murder?

# CHAPTER ONE

She reached out and touched his face as his steely grey eyes fixed on her. She felt him tense at her caress, but Lucy was glad he didn't draw away. Her fingers moved lightly over the craggy planes of his face, across the crow's feet at the corner of his eyes, tracing the fine lines of his cheekbones.

"You are beautiful," she whispered, and a strange look came into his eyes.

"Dear one, you are so young," his voice shook with emotion. "If you agree to this, know that I will strive to make you happy." He took her hand and kissed the back of her fingers. "But I know that my age may prevent you from ever loving me the way I would wish to be loved."

"I don't see age," Lucy said, her blue eyes serious, her tone fervent. "I see experience; I see adventure; I see so much I could learn from. Surely love—real love—is based on more than a number?"

He stared at her for a long moment, then nodded. "Then it is settled."

"Yes," Lucy said, drawing near to him, "It is settled. I am yours, Thornton. Yours." And she pressed her lips gently to his...

"Cut. Okay, that's good. Let's move on." Cosimo DeLuca's voice was weary and the dark circles under his eyes obvious. Biba May shot the director a quick glance as she moved in to drape a robe around Stella's shoulders, but Cosimo was lost in his notes already.

Stella, her blonde hair piled up under a 1920s Marcel Wave wig, glared at Biba. "I'm freezing. Be a bit quicker next time."

Biba said nothing. She'd learned a long time ago that rising to Stella's bait was never a good idea. Instead, she would just fix her dark brown eyes on the actress, and Stella would smirk. Biba never understood why Stella kept requesting her to be her assistant on set but, despite her bitchiness, Stella paid very well and having the odd cell phone thrown at her head was worth it. Besides, the second time Stella had gotten physical, Biba picked up the vase Stella had just hurled at her—and had thrown it right back, missing deliberately by an inch or so. Stella had been shocked…and then had burst into peals of laughter. "Quid pro quo, Biba May."

Biba knew Stella liked her feistiness and the fact that she, Stella, could go on a full-blown rant, and Biba would listen to it all and then tell her exactly what she thought, whether Stella liked it or not.

Which wasn't to say Stella liked Biba or anyone else, for that matter. Stella Reckless was the world's biggest movie star, a staggering beautiful blonde with curves to die for, a wide smile that could break into the most infectious laughter. Stella didn't give a fuck what people thought of her, rarely did anything for charity unless she got something out of it, and surrounded herself with her 'squad'—a flotilla of easily replaceable minor actresses and pretty boys who never said boo to her and instead kissed her ass to the press.

Except Biba. Biba wouldn't take any of her crap. An army brat, Biba May was used to tough people: her African American father, a hulking giant at nearly seven feet, was an army general, and her Creole mother was a major in the I Corps at the Joint Base Lewis–McChord just outside Tacoma. Biba had every intention of following her mother into the military until it was discovered at age fifteen that she had a heart murmur. After a failed surgery, Biba had spent her lengthy recovery watching old movies and falling in love with them, and she decided to pursue work as an assistant on movie sets. There she found a world where she could observe the inner workings of film and movie magic. Her natural efficiency and organizational skills had easily found a home behind the camera.

Often though, she was asked why she herself didn't want to act. Biba rolled her eyes, aware of why they asked her. She knew people considered her beautiful—her gorgeously clear caramel skin, large dark eyes, short cropped black hair and curvy, petite figure drew admirers constantly, but she insisted on resolutely downplaying her physical beauty.

"Hey." Someone nudged her now, and she turned to see her friend—her best friend as it turned out—Reggie, grinning at her. "You were out of it. Did Madame Lash need her ass kissed?"

Biba chuckled. "If she did, she came to the wrong person." She looked around. "They setting up the next scene?"

Reggie, who was the cowriter of the film, nodded at Cosimo DeLuca, who was still reading his notes and talking in a low voice to his director of photography. "You met him yet?"

Biba shook her head. "Not yet. He seems…sad. I didn't want to intrude by introducing myself. I mean, what does he care about a personal assistant?"

Reggie half-smiled. "Actually, he's one of the good ones. Cares about everyone. Too much, I think, sometimes."

"You know him well?"

"Not well, but I've worked with him a few times these past two years. His wife died a couple of years ago."

Biba looked at the director. "So that's what it is."

"What?"

"The sadness. How did she die?"

"She was sick, I think. Died young, too, she was only thirty-three. They had a kid, too. Nicco. He lives with his grandmother in Seattle. Doesn't see his dad much."

Biba shook her head. "That's terrible. Poor guy."

Reggie moved away, and Biba took a moment to study the director. He was devastatingly handsome, or he would be if he didn't wear his grief across every cell of his body. His dark curls were in disarray, there were purple shadows under his bright green eyes, and his thick brows were knotted and brooding. Biba's eyes dropped down to his mouth, his lips, and found the curve of them sensual and appealing.

She realized that she was staring just as Cosimo looked up and met her gaze. A jolt of adrenaline—and of desire—shot through her stomach, and she looked away, embarrassed. Luckily, Stella grabbed her at that moment, and she was kept too busy for the next hour to process why she had felt such a shift in her soul when DeLuca looked at her.

THEY WERE FILMING at Lakewood Manor, a gorgeous Tudor-type Gothic house just outside of Tacoma, Washington—Biba's hometown. So, she asked herself later as she trudged to Stella's trailer, why haven't you been home, May? She had made excuses to herself over the three days they had been in Washington, such as: they had only been there three days, things were always hectic at the beginning of a shoot and… and… and…

The truth was…she didn't want to go home only to be made to feel like a child again. Her mother had never been the warmest person, and Biba's father, with his fragile male ego, had taken his insecurities out on Biba from a young age. He could barely talk to her as an adult, but if Biba dared to get annoyed by it, Travis May would get verbally aggressive.

Biba loathed the idea of seeing him, not wanting to feel that sense of rage, betrayal, and injustice that her father kindled in her. Her mother...Biba had always felt that she was just an inconvenience to her mom, to their lives. She would never side with Biba over her father's behavior.

Biba blew out her cheeks as she knocked at Stella's trailer door and went in without waiting for a response. She felt the trailer moving and rolled her eyes. Stella must be in the bedroom with Damon.

Damon Tracy—or 'Prick Tracy' as he was called by the crew—was Stella's latest paramour—not that Stella cared much for him. Biba hated Damon—he was as bland as a beige wall and as dumb as a bag of hammers, but he thought himself wildly appealing to the opposite sex—and had, on more than one occasion, flirted with Biba, his eyes roaming freely over her body. He had a habit of cornering her suggestively with seemingly innocent requests. Biba gave him short shrift, but that just seemed to encourage him.

Stella's last boyfriend had been a sweetheart—Sasha, a businessman from Portland—and Stella had sent Biba to break up with him. Biba had been horrified and had burst into tears as Sasha took the news stoically, something she rarely did. Sasha had in turn comforted her, and they had remained good friends.

Damon? Biba would happily dump his ass for Stella, and knowing her boss, that day wasn't far off.

The trailer stopped rocking now, and to Biba's amusement, she heard Stella say, "Is that it? Jesus..."

Biba stifled a snort of laughter, but she didn't hide her grin when Damon stomped out of the bedroom in his shorts, shooting her a glare as he pulled his jeans on and disappeared out the door. Stella appeared a moment later, seeing Biba's grin. She shrugged. "Doesn't hurt to make him think he needs to up his game."

Biba grimaced. "Rather you than me."

Stella chuckled darkly. "I don't think there's much mileage left in Damon and I. Besides, I've got my eye on a much bigger prize."

"God, who now?"

Stella grinned at Biba's sarcastic tone. "Our delectable director, of course. You must have noticed how damn sexy that man is. God, Italian, too... I bet he fucks like an animal."

Biba turned her face away, not wanting Stella to see how utterly thrilling that thought was to her. "He's still mourning his wife, Stella. You might want to tread a little carefully."

Stella made a noise. "Please. This is the movie business. I bet he was screwing his leading ladies the second the wife was put in the ground."

She had a point, but somehow, Biba didn't think Cosimo DeLuca was like other men. She changed the subject. "Want to go over tomorrow's lines?"

Stella shrugged. "Sure. Then you can help me with a plan to seduce Cosimo. That man isn't leaving Washington without being fucked by me."

SEX WAS the last thing on Cosimo's mind. He went through the day's filming with his DP, Channing, and his assistant director and co-producer, Lars, but he couldn't concentrate on anything. This movie wasn't his first choice to make, but at least he had close friends on the crew, friends that understood that his priority, ever since Grace's death, was to try to find common ground with Nicco, their sixteen-year-old son.

Cosimo tapped his phone's screen and raised it to his ear. "Hey, Mom."

Olivia DeLuca's voice was warm. "Cos, how lovely to hear from you. How's filming?"

"First day. Always a strange one. We're shooting out of sequence, so the actors and crew haven't built up that chemistry yet. Same old, same old. How's Nicco?"

"Well...he likes his school, so that's something. After that trouble at Olympia High, I thought we would never get him settled. Just a shame we had to go private to find his niche."

"I'd pay any amount for that, Mom, so please don't worry." He hesitated. "I don't suppose he wants to speak to his dad today?"

Olivia sighed. "I'll see, Cos, but don't hold your breath."

There was a long pause, and then Cosimo heard his son pick up the phone. "Yo."

Cosimo, relieved, chuckled. "Yo back to you, too. How's things?"

"Cool. School's good."

"Glad to hear it. What's been going on?"

"Not much. Playing some football."

Cosimo was surprised. "Really?"

Nicco gave a mirthless laugh. "Yeah, Dad. Surprise, surprise, your son's good at something."

Cosimo's hands curled into fists. Here we go... "Nic, I've never thought you were bad at anything."

"I don't know, I'm a pretty shitty son."

"You are not." Nicco had been like this since his mother had died. They'd kept a lot of Grace's illness away from Nicco, and when she had died so unexpectedly, Nicco had been away on a school trip. The last time he'd talked to Grace, he'd been distracted and had gotten irritated with her fussing—what he called fussing—over him and had snapped at her. He'd never forgiven himself for that—and he'd never forgiven Cosimo for keeping the severity of Grace's illness from him. Cosimo felt the pain of that perceived betrayal every time he talked to or saw Nicco. He was losing his son, and he knew it.

"Whatever, Dad. How's the filming?"

"Just got started. You know, if you wanted, you could come down here on the weekend, hang out, see what we do?"

There was a long pause. "I have a game this weekend."

"Then I'll come to you." Cosimo had filming scheduled for both days, but he would let Channing direct them.

"Nah, you have work." Nicco hesitated. "Maybe the weekend after, I could come down on the bus."

"I'd like that." Cosimo felt a wave of hope flow through him. "Love you, buddy."

"Yeah." Nicco's voice had gone cold again. "Later, Dad."

"Later, Nic."

Cosimo heard the phone being handed back to his mother. Only Olivia DeLuca would still insist on a landline. "Hello, darling."

"Hey, Mom. Nic says he might come down the weekend after next."

"I heard. That's wonderful, Cos." There was a long pause. "Cosimo...try to be happy, son. I worry that you're going into one of your hermit phases. I worry you'll get depressed again."

Cosimo rubbed his eyes. "I'm fine, Mom, honestly. It's been two years, that's all. I want to know how to move past it, but I'm stuck at the moment. It'll work out."

"Open your heart again, son," Olivia said in a soft voice. "Grace would want you to find love again."

"I know. Thanks, Mom."

AFTER HE HUNG UP, he half-heartedly made some notes before

going out in the twilight down to the lake. The mansion was built alongside one of the biggest lakes in the area and the surrounding area was tranquil this late in the evening. Cosimo breathed in the night air, the sharp cold of it revitalizing his senses. It really was a beautiful place to film. The estate itself had been converted into a bed-and-breakfast some years ago and refurbished to an exquisite standard. The movie studio had bought out the rooms for the duration of the shoot, and some of the cast and crew were staying in the bedrooms that weren't used for filming. Cosimo looked back at the mansion now, lit up and warm. He knew he should be grateful for this job, and he was—he loved directing—but lately, he had been craving more solitude. Maybe his mom was right—he was becoming a grumpy old hermit again.

He shook his head and began to walk down to sit at the lake's edge. He heard a dog bark and looked around to see a German Shepard, one he recognized as the caretaker's dog, bounding around a slight figure who was brandishing a tree branch. The other end was in the dog's mouth, and they were playing tug-o-war with it. He heard the woman laughing and pretending to growl at the dog, and squinting through the gloom, he recognized Stella's personal assistant—Biba? Was that her name?—teasing the dog, and then rolling and playing with it on the grass.

Cosimo smiled. Sweet. He watched for a few minutes from his lakeside seat. The girl saw him as she was about to turn and go back inside. For a long moment they gazed at each other, reading the other's expression, and he saw her give him a slightly embarrassed wave. He raised his hand to wave back, but she had already turned to go back inside.

Cosimo turned back to the lake, but his mind remained on the young woman. He knew Stella Reckless was a mean boss, but this girl seemed to have the measure of her, and that intrigued him. He also knew Stella had been batting her eyes at him for the last three days, and he really didn't want to go there. Stella Reckless was not his type at all—he preferred nerds, like him—girls that would talk to him about something other than Hollywood, parties, or the Kardashians. Grace had been the biggest science geek and had been applying to NASA when she got sick.

He sighed and got up, walking slowly back to the mansion. His mom might be on him to find someone new, but Cosimo knew—she would have to be very special indeed.

HE WATCHED the director walk back to the mansion before slipping back into the woods. He'd been delighted when he discovered they'd been filming here. Open woods, the lake—these would all make it easier for him to get closer to Stella. Soon, he would contact her and make it known that he was there for her —in every way a man could be there for a beautiful woman like Stella Reckless. No one would stand in their way of their epic, once-in-a-lifetime love story...and God help anyone that tried...

2
-----

## CHAPTER TWO

"Beebs, come on. A half hour won't make any difference." Rich Furlough, one of the movie set's security guards openly sulked at Biba, who grinned back at him. Rich, and his joined-at-the-hip colleague Gunter, were some of her favorite people on any of the movies she'd worked on. Superb at their jobs, they had an irreverent and sometimes mutinous sense of fun. Rich, whose dark good looks and bright blue eyes could have made him a contender for stardom easily, was the instigator, always looking for ways to bring the more diva-like actors down to earth with a bump, and Gunter, a German-born bodybuilder, tagged along pondering the most random things in life, such as why dragonflies had multi-colored wings ("Zay are fancy-schmancy, no? Like 'zay are going to a party, ja?").

Biba adored both of them—the two men had been best friends since their college years, and in turn, they had taken her under their wing early on in her career. Gunter had a crush on Stella which remained resolutely unrequited, and so sometimes he would get drunk and wax mournfully about his 'lost love'.

Rich flirted outrageously with Biba, but they shared an almost fraternal bond, and now he was trying to persuade her to prank Damon, who Rich loathed. "Come on, Biba," he said again, his voice wheedling. "You know you want to."

"I'm not Krazy Gluing his moustache," Biba said firmly, trying and failing to keep a grin off her face. "Lila will kill me for ruining her makeup job on him."

Rich snorted. "He needs it." Biba winked at him and went to find her boss.

Stella was tapping her cigarette on the table in the trailer, her eyes locked in the middle distance. For a moment she didn't see Biba come in, then, after Biba had gotten tired of saying good morning and being ignored, she rapped on the table loudly.

"Hey, Spacecakes. Makeup in five."

Stella blinked, then smiled. "I heard you. Have you seen Damon this morning?"

"No, thank God." Biba stopped and narrowed her eyes at Stella. She knew this look of old. "Oh, no. I know what you're thinking."

"What?" Stella was all innocence.

"You get this look on your face when you're gearing up to dump someone. As much as I detest Damon, you can dump him yourself this time."

"I didn't ask you to do anything."

"No, but you will." Biba busied herself with the new script pages that had arrived. She frowned. "Are the new pages pink or yellow? Shit, I can't remember."

Stella ignored her. "Now that you mention Damon…"

"I didn't, you did."

Stella waved her cigarette at Biba, then lit it finally, blowing the smoke away from her assistant. It was one of the few courtesies she showed. "Perhaps it is time we went our separate ways."

"Hallelujah."

Stella studied her. "You really don't like him, do you? What's the matter, Beebs? Hate sharing me?"

"Always," Biba grinned sarcastically, and Stella laughed. "No, he's just a creep. You could do better."

Stella looked vaguely surprised at the compliment but didn't say anything. "Well...next time, I will. Our gorgeous director for one thing. Cosimo DeLuca...can you imagine getting reamed by that man? I bet he's packing, too."

Biba didn't answer, but the thought of Cosimo naked wasn't unpleasant—quite the opposite. Not that she'd ever tell Stella that. She remembered last night when she'd seen him watching her play with the caretaker's dog. He had looked almost...happy, enjoying watching the fun she was having with the German Shepard. Maybe he was a dog lover? That made him even more appealing. She pushed the thought of him away. Do not get a crush on him. Do not. It was ridiculous, anyway. She'd never spoken a word to him. When she'd given him that awkward wave last night, he'd looked so surprised that she had turned away, embarrassed, and almost run back to the manor house.

"Hey, Spacecakes," Stella's tone was annoyed, "Are you listening?"

"Sure."

"See if you can get a read on DeLuca's attitude toward me."

"How?"

"Watch him when I'm acting. See if he reacts...in an admiring way."

Biba started to grin. "So, if he..." She pretended to grab her crotch and gyrate, making an obscene gesture with her hand. Stella cackled with laughter. She could always be won over with a dirty joke.

"A little subtler than that, but yes." Stella stretched out her long legs and bunched her long blonde hair up into a ponytail. "Right. Makeup."

. . .

AFTER STELLA HAD LEFT her alone, Biba tidied up the trailer and got out Stella's clothes for later, hanging them and steaming the wrinkles out of them. When she was done, she went to the craft service trailer and grabbed some granola and coffee.

As she sat down, she felt someone tickle her sides and knew who it was. "Reginald." She said in an imperious voice then grinned as he sat down beside her. Reggie kissed her forehead.

"Good morning, beautiful." He immediately stole a spoonful of granola, his eyes twinkling behind his glasses, his thick, wavy blonde hair a mess as always.

"Reggie, the food is right there," she moaned, but really, she didn't mind. Reggie Quinn, screenwriter, music buff, fellow geek, was her best friend in the world, her 'person', the one she called at the highest points of her life and at the lowest.

He had been the one to get her the job of Stella's assistant in the first place. They'd met when he came to her college to give a lecture on working in the movie business and found Biba the only student willing to engage. He called her over afterward, and they'd talked long into the night at her favorite bar. They found so much common ground that they both joked that it had been love at first sight.

Their friendship, however, had remained platonic from the start. Biba never sought out romantic entanglements, and Reggie seemed too happy being single. Both of them agreed they had far better things to do with their lives. And Reggie was her champion when it came to her writing, endlessly giving her feedback and encouraging her to submit her work to agents. Biba still didn't believe she would ever make it as a screenwriter, but she was grateful to Reggie's support in any case.

Reggie balanced his chin on her shoulder, and she leaned her head against his. "How's the Wicked Witch?"

Biba grinned. "Okay at the moment. She has a new plan."

"Oh God. Who this time?" Reggie was rolling his eyes.

"Cosimo DeLuca."

"God," Reggie said, "Poor guy doesn't stand a chance."

"Right?" But suddenly Biba didn't want to talk about Stella seducing Cosimo—it gave her a weird, unfamiliar sensation of jealousy and pain that she didn't understand.

She finished her breakfast and said goodbye to Reggie, heading toward the makeup trailer.

As she rounded the corner, she suddenly rocked back, almost colliding with someone. When she saw who it was, her heart thumped against her ribs.

Cosimo looked startled, then he smiled, and to Biba, it felt like the sun had come out. "Hello at last." His voice was deep and rich, only a hint of an accent, but it sent her senses reeling.

At last? That made her stomach flutter. "Hello, Mr. DeLuca, it's good to meet you." Not knowing what to do, she stuck her hand out, and his big, warm, dry hand closed around hers.

There was a long hesitation as they both stared at each other, and Biba felt herself reddening. His eyes were intensely fixed on hers—such a beautiful green—and his lashes were thick and black and long. When his eyes dropped to her full lips for a second, Biba felt a thrill go through her. God, he really was drop-dead gorgeous...and he was making her body feel things she'd never felt.

"It's Biba, isn't it?"

She nodded, feeling breathless. He smiled at her. "My mom used to model for Biba in London in the Sixties. Lovely name."

"Thank you. Is there anything I can do for you, Mr. DeLuca?" Like kiss you? Like run my hand through that gloriously wild mop of curls on your handsome head?

Cosimo smiled. "You're very kind, but no, thank you. And it's

Cosimo, Biba. Are you looking for Ms. Reckless? I believe I saw her walking back to her trailer."

"Thanks." She smiled at him and was gratified to see him nod. There were two rosy spots on his cheeks that surprised her—but maybe the guy was just really shy. She had heard that about him and so far, she'd seen no evidence to contradict it.

He also seemed in no hurry to leave her side. "How are you enjoying the shoot? Not that we've been here long, but..."

Cosimo was interrupted by the hasty arrival of Rich, who shoved something into Biba's hand and ran off, shouting "Sorry, Beebs!"

Both Biba and Cosimo looked at each other askance, then Biba looked down. A half-empty tube of Krazy Glue.

"What was that about?" Cosimo looked after the retreating—and laughing—form of Rich.

Biba shook her head. She didn't want to get Rich into trouble. "Nothing. Sorry, Mr— Cosimo. I do have to get to Stella."

"Of course. Again, good to talk to you, Biba." He smiled and touched her arm before he moved away. Biba took a long shaky breath in. Her skin burned where he'd touched it, and she wondered how her body would feel with his hands on it, stroking her, caressing her...

Jesus. A steady pulse beat between her legs, and she had to take a moment to collect herself.

LATER, watching the scene between Stella and Damon on the set, Biba couldn't help but watch how Cosimo reacted to his actors. He was unfailingly polite, but knew what he wanted, explaining to them both carefully how he felt the scene should be played, but listening to their suggestions. Gentle, she thought to herself. He's a gentle man.

Damon was fiddling with his moustache, scratching the skin

around it, and Stella looked annoyed. "I don't want flaky skin in my mouth, Damon, thank you very much."

Damon ignored her. "So damn itchy."

"God, haven't you ever had fake hair put on?" Stella eyed his hairline. "Looks like you'll need to in a couple of years, anyway."

"Don't be a bitch." Damon poked a finger into the moustache. "My lip feels numb."

Oh God. Biba's hand went into her jeans pocket to feel the tube of Krazy Glue. She shot a look over at Rich, who deliberately wasn't looking at her. Oh fuck.

Her fears were realized a half-hour later, when in the middle of a kissing scene, Stella broke away from Damon. "Eww, what is that?"

"Whath whath?" Damon's speech was lispy and slurred, and he poked at his upper lip again. "Whath the thuck?" He tore the moustache off, making everyone wince and his lip bleed.

"Oh, dear God." Stella was both repulsed and amused—Damon's lip was three times the size it should have been. He looked like a duck.

## 3
# CHAPTER THREE

Biba paled. Damon was obviously allergic to the Krazy Glue Rich had put on the fake hair. She moved behind the security guard and prodded him hard in the back. "You idiot. Look what you've done," she hissed at him.

"How was I to know he's allergic?" There was no guilt in Rich's voice, and instead, he moved forward. "Hey, everyone, calm down. Anyone got an EpiPen? We might need it. In the meantime, I'll call medical."

Cosimo sighed, his schedule out of whack now, his concentration broken. "Okay, people, that's a wrap for today. Damon, go get treatment." He turned and caught Biba's eye, and she was astonished to see him smirk and wink at her. Clearly, Cosimo had no time for divas either.

BIBA CAUGHT up with Rich later and punched his chest hard. Rich grinned. "Sorry I dumped the glue on you, Beebs. I had to make a quick getaway."

"And frame me, you asshole."

"You know, in some war zones, Krazy Glue is used to close

wounds," Gunter said thoughtfully. "Maybe Biba should seal up your wing wang as punishment." He bit into an apple nonchalantly as both Biba and Rich stared at him.

"Thanks, guy." Rich said as Biba started to laugh.

"Maybe that's a great idea," Biba pretended to reach for Rich's fly. "Come hold him down, Gunter, while I…"

Rich skipped out of her reach. "Ha ha. Listen, in all seriousness, I am sorry. If Cosimo says anything, tell him it was me."

"Oh, I will," Biba said. "I have no trouble ratting you out, you douche."

Rich grinned. "You love me really."

"Nah."

"Yup. If I wasn't so busy working, you'd be all over me. You're insatiable."

Biba started to laugh. Rich's teasing was something she found entirely funny, mostly because he did it in such an open and non-creepy way. "Rich, I've told you before. I like big bratwurst, not chipolatas."

Gunter looked up eagerly. "You like ze German bratwurst?"

Biba grinned and didn't answer. Rich sighed and slumped on the sofa in his trailer. "Well, that was fun. What should we do tomorrow?"

Biba kicked his feet as she passed him on her way out. "How about your job? Random, I know."

"Tyrant."

"Lazy bitch."

Rich grinned. "Later, boo."

"Later. Bye, Gun."

"Goodbye, Bratwurst Princess."

Biba was still grinning as she went to find Stella, who was in a good mood. "I heard that was you with the Krazy Glue." She actually hugged Biba, who rocked back a little at the unexpected embrace. "Well done."

Biba extracted herself. "Well, you heard wrong. Not that Prick Tracy didn't deserve it, but I wouldn't wish that...duck pout...on anyone." She smirked a little, and Stella grinned.

"Right?" Stella cackled gleefully. She sat down, opening the mini-fridge and taking out a beer. She never thought to offer Biba one, but Biba was used to it. "God, what a day. And...what a night I have planned."

She waggled her eyebrows at Biba, who knew Stella wanted her to ask about it. Sighing, she pandered to her boss's wishes. "How so?"

"What I like to call the first offensive of the 'Make Cosimo Mine' campaign. We're meeting later to discuss the script and my character's motivation." She took a swig of beer and licked her lips slowly. "My character motivation being 'I want to suck your big dick, Mr. Director'." She snorted with laughter, but Biba felt a strange pang of jealousy.

"Stella...just a warning. The dude doesn't seem the type to... have on-set dalliances. He's pretty shy."

Stella looked askance at her. "And you know him so well because...?"

"I don't. It's just the impression I get."

Stella shrugged. She stood and pulled open her robe. "He'll stop being so shy when he sees this." Stella wasn't shy about showing off her stunning figure: her full breasts, trim stomach, and long, long legs. Biba had seen it all before.

"Whatever you say. Listen, you got everything you need? I'm going to take off."

"Yes, fine. Four a.m. call tomorrow. Be here at three-thirty, please."

Biba groaned. "God. That's not even a real time. You made it up." But she was amazed by the 'please'. Stella grinned at her joke.

"Believe me, I'd rather sleep in until noon, too, but we have to film some scenes with the early morning light." She finally stopped and looked at Biba. "Get some rest. You look exhausted."

Jesus, what was going on with Stella? She was never this nice unless...ah, yes. Biba remembered now. Stella was always in a better mood when she was about to seduce someone. Biba didn't usually care...and she questioned herself why she did now.

"Fine. See you in the morning."

BIBA DEBATED whether to go borrow the caretaker's dog again and go down to the lake—to walk the dog, she told herself, not to see if Cosimo would be there—but she was tired. Instead she went to find Reggie.

Weaving in between the trailers, she noticed it had gotten really dark just moments before she stumbled over some loose ground. She crashed down onto her knees, then gasped in pain as her right knee crunched against a stone. "Oww, oww, fucking ouch, ouch..." She cursed some more as she clambered to her feet and tested her knee. It wasn't broken, but it still hurt like hell.

Biba limped towards the manor house, but as she reached the end of the line of trailers, someone stepped out in front of her and blocked her way—and the light. Biba stepped back sharply in surprise, and then her pulse began to beat painfully as the figure reached for her. Seizing her by the shoulders, her assailant slammed her back hard against the last trailer.

COSIMO CHATTED with Channing and Lars for a while, and then debated whether to go get some food. Deciding he wasn't hungry, instead he texted Nicco to tell him he had arranged a car to collect him and bring him to the set the weekend after next.

He waited for a reply, not expecting one so soon, but when his phone beeped, he hated the pathetic excitement he felt. It was only a text message, for Chrissakes. His pleasure soon dissipated when he saw Nicco's reply.

Cool.

That was it. Better than nothing, Cosimo thought, his heart sinking. What the hell would that weekend be like with a monosyllabic teen in tow? Shit. Maybe he should have thought it through a little more. He wondered if he could persuade some of the younger members of the crew to help him out, help him find common ground. Rich and Gunter certainly would help—Nicco would find their antics fun and cool. ...And what about Biba? She couldn't be more than twenty-two or -three at the most.

God. So young. Cosimo was feeling every one of his forty years lately. Today, although he couldn't really sanction the loss of his supporting actor for even one day, he'd finally been shaken out of the listlessness he'd been feeling by laughter. God, he missed just hanging loose and laughing at silly stuff, anything, a dumb TV show, or just friends being goofy. He had seen the friendship, the kinship between Biba, Rich, and Gunter —also Biba's deep friendship with Reggie Quinn, the geeky, sweet—and Cosimo presumed, gay—cowriter of the film. He envied them the trust they had between each other, the connection.

When Grace had died, he had let the friendships they'd shared slip away, unable to spend time with the people who had known them as a couple. It was just too damn painful. But now, he wished he'd tried more. Maybe he should call one or two of them and test the water.

You sound like such a sad sack. Cosimo sighed and grabbed his pack of cigarettes. He swore to Olivia he would quit smoking before he was forty, but he would have one at night, just to relax and decompress.

He walked out into the night air, turned towards the lake... and heard her scream.

A HAND CLAMPED over her mouth and the man's body pressed hard against hers. Biba's panic made it hard for her to identify her attacker until he spoke.

"You little cunt." Damon. Oh God. "I know it was you with the Krazy Glue. What the fuck did you think you were doing?"

"It wasn't me! Now get your filthy hands off me!" She tried to push him away, but he was twice the size of her and the product of steroids. He shoved her harder into the trailer wall.

"No, I don't think I will. Not until you've made it up to me, and since Stella seems to have shut me out, you can take her place."

Biba was terrified as Damon tugged her jeans down to midthigh. "No, no, no..." She wriggled and panicked, but he covered her mouth as he stuck his hand between her legs.

"Come on, beauty, give it up. I know you're not fucking that little cocksucker Quinn, so what's the difference?"

He was tearing at her panties now. Biba bit down hard on his hand, and as he released her with a pained shout, she screamed at the top of her lungs. Damon, raging now, cuffed her viciously on the face, and Biba slumped to the ground. In an instant he was on her, and she felt the warm flesh of his penis against her bare thigh. No! No way, this wasn't happening!

"Please! Stop! No, I don't want this..."

"I don't give a fuck if you don't want it, you little cunt. Who the hell are you to decide? Open your damn legs."

Biba clamped her thighs tighter together, and Damon, growling, punched her hard in the stomach. All the air was pushed from her lungs as she gasped in pain, and then Damon pushed her legs apart and started to push inside her.

Then, from out of nowhere a whirlwind of rage and fury yanked Damon up and threw him bodily across the ground away from Biba, and then gentle arms were wrapping a coat around her.

"It's okay, sweetheart, we've got you. Rich, Gunter, detain this asshole until the police get here. Reggie, go call the police…I'll take care of Biba."

Through the fog of shock and terror, Biba realized it was Cosimo holding her so tenderly. She couldn't help but nestle into the comfort and safety of his arms. He picked her up and carried her into the manor house. The owner of the house took one look at Biba and rushed to help.

"Let's take her to the Lakewood Suite," her gentle voice said, "the bed's comfortable, and there's a fire going. I'll make some tea."

Cosimo carried her into the room as if she weighed nothing and set her down onto the counterpane. Biba panicked at the thought of him leaving her, but as he tucked the sheet around her, he stayed, his arms wrapped around her.

"It's okay, sweetheart. The police will be here soon, and we'll get you checked out by a doctor." He was stroking her hair away from her face, and she felt his lips press against her temple.

Biba let the shock and terror seep from her bones. "I'm so sorry, Cosimo," she said, "I didn't see him coming."

"Don't worry, Biba. Damon won't ever bother you again if he wants to keep his career. He should be in jail. Did he hurt you?"

She nodded. "But he didn't… I mean, I didn't let him…" She couldn't say the word 'rape' out loud.

Cosimo moved so he could study her face. "You did good. You did exactly what you were supposed to." There was a knock at the door and Cosimo looked at her. "Are you ready?"

She nodded. "Please don't leave me alone."

He leaned his forehead against hers. "Never," he whispered. "I'll never leave you."

And in that moment, they both knew something had changed irrevocably between them.

## CHAPTER FOUR

The police interview was harrowing, hearing Biba having to relive what just happened. Damon was arrested, but the police warned them that with his connections and his money, he would be out on bail soon. Cosimo assured the police that security on set would be upped. "He won't get near anyone here," he said, his voice like stone.

He called Rich and Gunter to him, and, after giving them an ass-kicking for dragging Biba into their antics, he told them to hire some more security. "Any sign of Tracy, he's toast, you understand?"

Both Rich and Gunter looked shell-shocked by the evening's events. Rich looked past his boss to the closed door of the suite. "Can we go see Biba? I need to apologize."

Cosimo shook his head. "The doctor is in with her...he's... collecting evidence."

Both Gunter and Rich's faces looked as sickened as Cosimo felt. "Mein Gott." Gunter shook his head, and Cosimo sighed.

"I think she needs some peace and quiet."

No sooner were the words out of his mouth when Stella came crashing into the room, her robes and scarves flying, her face pale—but still beautifully made up. "Cosimo, thank God." She put her hands on his chest and gazed into his eyes. "How is she? Is she badly hurt? Are you?"

Cosimo extracted himself from Stella's grip and gently pushed her away. "Biba's going to be fine. She just needs rest and T.L.C. for a day or two. Will you cope without her?" The way he framed it, the tone of his voice was very clear. You will cope without her whether you like it or not.

Stella had obviously decided to go with being magnanimous. "Of course, of course. Oh dear, what a terrible thing to happen. I blame myself."

Cosimo nodded his head at Rich and Gunter, at his signal, made their escape. Cosimo sat down, wishing he could smoke inside, and instead braced himself for Stella's drama.

Stella threw her hands out wide. "I knew he was trouble. I should have protected Biba, protected myself. I'm sorry, Cosimo. I really am."

Oh God, it was going to be a long night. "Stella...I think we've dealt with Damon now. There's no point in recriminations. Damon was the one to blame, no one else."

Stella picked at her nails. "Have you fired him?"

"Obviously. Luckily, we already had someone lined up in case we ran into trouble with Damon."

Stella smiled. "You obviously knew his reputation."

"He wasn't my first choice with this film. The studio wanted him. I think they wanted to capitalize on your off-screen relationship."

Stella laughed softly. "Such as it was. It was never serious, Cosimo, you know that. I wasn't ready to get serious about anyone until..." She slid her eyes demurely away from his. "Well..."

Cosimo had to stop himself from rolling his eyes. Luckily,

the next moment, the doctor came out from Biba's room. Cosimo stood to shake his hand.

"She'll be okay—physically, at least. Obviously, it's not my place to discuss my findings, so you'll have to ask Miss May. I have prescribed a sleeping tablet for tonight and advised her to take it. Just to make sure she gets some rest."

"Thank you, Doctor. I hope—"

"Can she have visitors?" Stella interrupted Cosimo, and the doctor finally noticed her. His eyes widened a little—obviously a little starstruck.

"Well...she did say only Mr. DeLuca or Mr. Quinn..."

"Then that's final," Cosimo said firmly. "Doctor, thank you." He waited until the doctor had gone before turning to Stella. "Stella, thank you, but I've got this from here. I'll let you know in the morning if anything changes."

Stella was about to argue, but at that moment, Reggie, breathless, fraught, came into the room. "Is she okay? Is Biba okay?"

Cosimo calmed him down. "You can go in," he said gently, patting his shoulder. "She wants to see you."

He nodded to Stella—a dismissal—and was relieved when she took the hint. "Let me know if you need anything." She touched his chest again, then left. Her scent, heavy and seductive, followed her, and Cosimo sighed.

He sat down heavily, finally alone, and tried to process the horror of what had happened. No doubt the studio would be outraged, but at least he could defend himself there. Damon had been their choice. They would scramble to spin the story how they wanted it, and they would want Cosimo and Biba to keep their mouths shut. Cosimo didn't care about himself, but if the studio decided she was replaceable...no. He would protect her until they backed off—that was a no-brainer. They didn't get to employ a rapist and then blame the victim. Fuck them.

Anger was roiling away inside him, but more than that, he couldn't stop hearing that scream—her panicked, soul-crushing scream. Biba struck him as someone who didn't scare easily, but the cry she gave was one of pure terror. God, poor kid.

He rubbed his eyes, drained. Fuck this world, fuck all the predators in it. He didn't care that now he would have to scrap a couple of days filming. He knew who he would call to replace Damon—his old friend Sifrido Tofaro. Sifrido was just making it in Hollywood after being an A-plus lister in Italian movies for over a decade—he would be perfect for the part of Henry in this thing. He'd call him in the morning.

Cosimo heard Reggie come out of Biba's room and looked up. "She okay?"

Reggie nodded, looking drawn. "Yeah, she'll be fine. Just shocked, I think. It...well...it's not the first time... Never mind. Look, thanks, Cosimo, truly. Thanks for looking out after her."

"Anytime."

Reggie nodded. "You staying up here?"

"For peace of mind."

Reggie smiled at him. "Cool. Biba's still awake if you want to go in. I know she wants to thank you herself."

"There's no need, but I'll go and say goodnight. Thanks, Reggie."

"See you in the morning."

BIBA HEARD the soft knock at the door, and her heart began to beat a little faster. "Come in."

She almost sighed with pleasure when Cosimo came in. God, the man was so freakin'...beautiful. That was the only word for him. The sedative the doctor had given her was kicking in, and her mind was a little swirly. She smiled at him. "Hello, again, savior."

His smile was sweet. "Nothing anyone else wouldn't have done. How are you feeling?"

She nodded. "Alright. A little dopey—the doctor gave me the good stuff."

Cosimo laughed. "Good, you deserve it. Look, take tomorrow off. Hell, take as long as you need off."

She held out her hand, and he took it, winding his fingers between hers as he sat on the side of the bed. His thumb stroked a gentle pattern over the back of her hand. "Thank you, Cosimo. I mean it."

Cosimo hesitated before tracing a finger down her cheek. "I'll never let anyone hurt you," he said, his voice breaking. "Damon is in jail. If he doesn't want to stay there, he'll never come near you or this set again, I promise." He sighed. "I'm so sorry this happened, Biba. I've already kicked Rich's ass."

Her eyes opened wide. "Please don't fire them."

"I won't, don't worry. Damon...was a ticking time bomb. Reggie tells me he was harassing you before."

"A little. Nothing I couldn't handle."

Cosimo smiled. "I believe you."

They gazed at each other, still holding hands. The silence stretched, but neither felt awkward. Finally, Cosimo, his eyes curious, gave a short laugh. "What is this happening here?"

Biba, her face burning, smiled. "I don't know. But I...I like it."

Cosimo stroked her hands. "Me, too."

God, she wanted to kiss him so badly, but she knew it would be wrong. He was her boss, and he'd just saved her from being raped or worse. "Friends is always a good start," she said quietly, and Cosimo nodded.

"God knows I could use a few."

Biba squeezed his hand. "I'm sorry about your wife, Cosimo. Reggie told me about her."

"Thanks, sweetheart. Hey, listen, my son is coming down

from Seattle in a week or so. He's...let's just say he's sixteen and not that fond of his dad at the moment. If you have any ideas on how to entertain him, I'm all ears."

Biba smiled. "I'll get thinking about it."

Cosimo nodded and reluctantly, it seemed, released her hand. He leaned forward and pressed his lips to her forehead. "Get some rest now, Beebs. See how you feel in the morning."

Her whole body was crying out for him to kiss her mouth, but he got up and left the room, shooting her a final, devastating smile before he closed the door behind him.

Biba lay back, feeling sleep begin to creep over her body. Her stomach ached where Damon had punched her, but she didn't care. She was okay. And she had a new friend.

In the moments before she fell asleep, she told herself she wasn't falling for Cosimo DeLuca, but she knew, deep down, that wasn't true.

# CHAPTER FIVE

In the morning, Biba woke, her head foggy from the sleeping tablet. She rolled over in bed and looked at the alarm clock. Five a.m. She lay back sighing. So much for the tablet. Her stomach growled, and she realized she was starving, her hunger probably what had woken her up. She slid from the bed and tugged a robe around herself. Opening the door to the suite, she was amazed to see Cosimo, sprawled in a chair, his head resting on his hand. He'd stayed.

Her emotions in turmoil, Biba crouched down by his side. "Cosimo?" Her voice was a whisper. He didn't move. Biba, her hand trembling, touched him, her hand resting on his stomach lightly. "Cosimo?"

Cosimo opened his eyes slowly and gazed at her. Biba was almost breathless. Cosimo's hand covered her hand resting on his stomach, but he stayed silent. Biba leaned in and kissed his mouth, just once, lightly...

His hands were in her hair then, his mouth rough against hers as he kissed her back, almost ferocious in his desire for her. As he stood, pulling her to her feet, he looked intently into her eyes. "Are you sure?"

Biba nodded, knowing this moment was the one where her life changed forever. In the bedroom, she pulled off his sweater, running her hands lightly over his hard chest. His hands were at the waistband of her jeans, and as they stripped, they kissed, lips demanding and hungry on the other's.

He laid her back on the bed and hitched her legs around his waist. "Biba..." he whispered

as he gently slid into her...

BIBA OPENED HER EYES. Damn. Oh, damn. What a dream to have now...and damn her subconscious for waking her up before she could imagine what it would be like to make love to Cosimo DeLuca. She pushed the sheets on the bed back, her body a bit cold and stiff. Her stomach ached badly and when she pulled her T-shirt up, she saw the bruised imprint of Damon's knuckles on her skin. Bastard.

Biba rolled out of bed, giving a little groan. It was still early, the pale blue light of dawn peeking through the window. Biba pulled her sneakers on and crept out of the room. Just like in her dream, Cosimo was asleep in an easy chair in the sitting room, and she smiled to herself. She found a wool throw and gently draped it on him. He looked like he needed the sleep, and she found herself longing to trace the violet shadows under his eyes with her fingertip.

She found a scrap of paper and hurriedly scribbled a note before he woke up.

COSIMO,

Thank you so much for what you did for me last night. I can never repay you.

I'm feeling much better today, so I'll be back at work. I'll try to think of some fun things you can do with your son.

Thank you again,

Biba.

BIBA PAUSED, then erased her name and wrote: Your friend, always, Biba. She balanced it on his stomach where she was sure it wouldn't fall off, resisting the temptation to stroke the hard muscle beneath the light cotton shirt, and left him to sleep.

SHE WALKED SLOWLY BACK to the trailers, wondering if she should go straight to Stella's—it must be nearly six a.m. already, and they had a seven a.m. call. She opened the door to the trailer to see Stella already awake and dressed. Biba half-smiled at her boss. "Hey."

"Hey, yourself." Stella studied her. "How are you feeling?"

"Sore, but otherwise fine. Did you want me to get some coffee?"

"I have it coming. Breakfast, for both of us."

Biba blinked. "What?"

Stella smiled. "I'm not a total bitch, Biba. You've been through a bad night. Come on, sit down. You're not working today."

Stella, of course, wouldn't be Stella unless she got the gossip on any situation, and so she made Biba tell her everything. To Biba's relief, Stella didn't linger on the attack, but rather how Cosimo acted afterwards.

"He was sweet," Biba told her, "sweet and professional." That was almost the truth. She still felt the touch of his hand on her cheek—the tenderness, the intimacy of the gesture—but she was damned if she'd share that detail with Stella.

She knew what Stella wanted, of course. She wanted to know if Cosimo had talked about her; she didn't care if Biba got to spend time with the director. It never occurred to Stella that Cosimo and Biba might share a connection, and the idea of an attraction between them would be laughable to the blonde movie star.

Biba was grateful for that fact. It meant Stella wouldn't be jealous or be a bitch if Cosimo and Biba were to talk. And, God, she wanted to talk to him, find out about him, his son, his life. She'd had a taste of what a friendship with him could be like, and Biba wanted more.

AFTER BREAKFAST, Stella appeared to forget she had given Biba the day off, but Biba was grateful for the list of chores Stella barked at her. Lazing around wasn't Biba's style, and the quicker she got back to work, she figured, the quicker her colleagues' fascination with what had happened would dissipate.

COSIMO WAS surprised when he saw Biba back at Stella's side on the set. He smiled at the young woman, and she grinned back. "You okay?" He mouthed to her, and she nodded, her sweet face lighting up.

Cosimo felt a shift inside him. Biba May was nearly half his age but there was something in her nature, her spirit, the way she dealt with Stella Reckless, that belied her young age. She was an old soul, like him. She was beautiful, but that wasn't what drew him to her. Cosimo had met, seen, even slept with some of the most beautiful women in the world and knew very well that beauty meant nothing at the end of it all. Kindness, intelligence, humor—that's what he looked for.

He stopped himself. Woah. He was thinking about what he

looked for in a woman? That was...progress. That's what Grace would have called it...progress. You would like Biba, Grace...but I wouldn't look for your approval now, and you wouldn't want me to. Can I really move on? Cosimo watched Biba move around with the crew, laughing and joking with them, but remaining efficient and responsible at the same time.

"Cos? You ready?" Lars, his assistant director, called over to him, and Cosimo switched back into director mode.

Filming went smoothly. The man playing 'Thornton', Stella's character Lucy's much older husband, was an Italian star, one who had made his name decades before Stella was even born. Franco Discali was an old-fashioned gentleman, respectful but flirtatious with the female members of crew. He had little time for diva antics, but he had taken a shine to Biba, and she in turn adored the older man. He was funny and erudite, and she loved talking to him about movies and his career.

Now, as he waited to film his next scene, he beckoned Biba over. "Buongiorno, Biba May."

Biba giggled. Franco always called her by her full name and Biba wasn't sure if it was because he thought it was her full name—like Biba-May Bloggs—or if he knew better and just liked using her full name. Franco was mischievous like that.

"Buongiorno, Franco. You got everything you need?"

"I'm fine. Wishing Stella would hurry up and read her lines. She seems to be flirting with Cosimo instead of acting."

Biba glanced over at Stella, who was rubbing her hand up and down Cosimo's arm. Biba looked away, trying to quell the stab of jealousy that made her stomach hurt. Still, she couldn't help but talk about Cosimo to Franco.

"You've worked with Cosimo before, right?"

"Many times since he started his career." There was a strange hint of paternal pride in Franco's voice. "I've never seen anyone with his vision before. I should have retired a decade ago, but I wanted to continue to work with him. I only act in Cosimo's films now."

Biba was touched. "He's a good guy."

"He is, he truly is. I knew his mother, you know, back in the day." Franco smiled at Biba. "You remind me of her."

"How so?"

"Your kindness. She would like you." Franco looked back at Stella, and his mouth twitched up in a smirk. "Unlike Ms. Reckless. She's not subtle, is she?"

Biba grinned. "Nope. Not in any way. In a strange way, I kind of admire her for saying what she wants."

"But there's no mystery, no allure." Franco studied her. "Cosimo told me what happened, Biba May. I'm so sorry."

Biba felt choked up, so she just nodded. "Thanks, Franco."

FILMING WENT SMOOTHLY for the rest of the day, and it wasn't until they broke for a meal that Rich came to find her. For once, his bright blue eyes were serious. "Beebs, I'm so sorry. I had no idea Damon would react like that."

Biba smiled at him. "Don't worry about it, Rich, really. He's gone; that's all that matters. Did Cosimo bawl you out?"

"And then some, but I deserved it." He smiled at her ruefully. "But he did tell me you asked him not to fire me. I'm grateful, Beebs, really."

Biba hugged him. Rich had a kind heart even if he was sometimes thoughtless. He squeezed her in his arms. They'd known each other long enough now, that they were as close as...

"Beebs?"

"Yup?"

"Maybe some night...I could take you out?"

Woah. Biba looked up at him. There was no denying he was utterly gorgeous, all dark hair and bright blue eyes and sexy smile...and she didn't mind him asking. She was flattered, but...

She shot a quick look at Cosimo. Out of your league, girl, and you know it. He's a grown man. You're just a kid. She smiled at Rich. "That would be fun...I do have to warn you that I'm, um...not looking for anything serious."

Rich grinned. "Me neither. Just thought we could have some fun."

The kind of fun Rich wanted wasn't what she was looking for either, but Biba thought she could be honest with him later. Rich wasn't threatening at all, and at least Biba felt safe with him in a way which she hadn't felt with anyone...ever.

Cosimo looked over at them now and smiled, and Biba's belly quivered with desire. Stop it. She gave him a half-smile then moved out of his line of vision. Yeah, you need to tell Rich it can't go anywhere. But the thought of a night out with fun-loving Rich was probably what she needed right now—and if something grew out of it, at least it would distract her from thinking about Cosimo DeLuca.

After dinner, Cosimo caught up to her as she was walking slowly to the trailers. "Hey."

Her skin trembled with pleasure, and she smiled up at him. Even his 'Hey' had so much intimacy in it. She wanted to fold herself into his arms, breath in his woody, spicy scent, press her mouth against his lips.

Jesus. Stop. "How are you feeling?"

She nodded. "I'm good, honestly. Stella's had me running everywhere, so I've not had time to sit and brood. Which is good."

Cosimo frowned a little. "But you've processed what happened?"

Biba didn't know how to answer him. "It happened. I can't... let it stop me."

His eyes were so serious, so intense on hers. "Sweet girl... maybe you should see a counselor? I'm worried about the PTSD aspect."

God, he was lovely. "I'm honestly okay, Cosimo, I swear. But I appreciate your concern."

Please touch me, please don't touch me. Biba couldn't look away from his gaze. Cosimo's fingers reach for her face, then dropped as if he realized what he was about to do. He looked away.

"There's a mist out on the lake. I'll be walking down there tonight about ten, if you and caretaker's dog are around. If you feel like talking."

Biba could see his cheeks were a little flushed, and she felt her own face burning. She nodded. "That sounds like something I could do." God, the whole thing was so awkward and yet intoxicating.

"Good. See you later then." He smiled, the corners of his eyes wrinkling, then he nodded and walked away. Biba stared after him. Why the hell did this man have such an effect on her? A pulse was beating steadily between her legs, and she wanted to go after him, wrap her legs around his waist and beg him to fuck her...

A cold shower. A very, very cold shower was what she needed now. She turned back and went back to her room.

HE WATCHED Biba May talking to Cosimo DeLuca. That was interesting. There was clearly something going on between them if the way they looked at each other was anything to go by.

Good. It would mean Stella's assistant would be distracted, and he could gain access to the blonde.

She haunted his dreams and had done so since he was a teenager. He didn't care that she was a lot older than him. Her smooth skin and icy-blue eyes made his groin tighten. Soon, he would bury his cock deep into her welcoming cunt, and she would tell him over and over how much she loved him. Then once filming was done, they would go away to his cabin down in the Oregon woods, and there, with his knife, he would show her how much she meant to him before he joined her in the forever world of death.

## CHAPTER SIX

It was darker tonight, the moon covered by clouds, as Biba walked down to the lake. She'd decided against bringing the dog, and she told herself it was because the dog would get bored if they sat around to do nothing but talk.

Cosimo's smile when she saw him made her heart soar. "Hey," she said shyly.

Cosimo nodded towards a little jetty a way along the shore. "It's private."

At the end of the jetty, there was a small bench, above which a lamp sputtered out weak light. Cosimo took his sweater off and draped it around Biba's shoulders when she shivered. The cream-colored muslin shirt he had on was slightly see-through, and Biba had to look away from the shape of his sculpted chest, the flat stomach, the indentation of his navel.

They sat down on the bench closely, her thigh resting against his. The mist hung around them in a ghostly white fog. Cosimo's arm was along the top of the bench, his fingers close to Biba's arm. If she moved just a little, it would be as if his arm was around her...

She felt breathless and shy. Cosimo was studying her. "It's beautiful here, isn't it?"

She nodded. "Gorgeous."

They gazed at each other. Cosmo's eyes were somber. "Biba... if you knew what was going through my mind right now...but, I'm so much older than you, and I'm your boss."

"I know. Not that much older than me."

Cosimo smiled slightly. "May I ask how old you are?"

Biba thought about adding a couple of years to her age, but she knew she couldn't lie to this man. "Twenty-two."

He groaned, and she chuckled. "Cosimo, you can't be older than..." Then she remembered he had a sixteen-year-old son. "You must have had Nicco very young. Barely a teen."

Cosimo laughed, his smile lighting up his face. "God, you're nearer his age than mine and..."

Biba moved in and pressed her lips to his, unable to hold back any longer. Cosimo kissed her back, his fingers sliding into her hair, his lips tender against hers. When they broke away, they were both breathless. Cosimo closed his eyes and leaned his forehead against hers. "We shouldn't have done that...but, God, I'm glad we did."

Biba cradled his face in her palms. "I've been dreaming about it since last night."

"Me, too. I'm just scared it makes me an old pervert."

They both laughed. "Well, then I'm a young pervert. I just wanted to touch you so badly."

Cosimo took her hand and pressed it against his chest, over his heart. "Feel that? It hasn't beat like that since..."

"Since Grace." Biba nodded, comfortable talking about Cosimo's wife. "I'm honored."

Her hands shaking, she brought his to her chest, his big hand cupping her left breast. Cosimo stroked his thumb across her nipple, and Biba shivered. She stepped away from him and pulled her T-shirt over her head as Cosimo watched her, then straddled his lap. His arms snaked around her waist, stroked her back as he gazed at her caramel skin, her full breasts, the soft curve of her belly. "God, you're beautiful," he whispered. Biba tangled her fingers in his dark curls.

"I want you so badly."

With a growl he answered her and lowered her down onto the cold wooden planks of the jetty, covering her body with his. He kissed her lips, moving down to her throat, trailing his kisses down the valley between her breasts, then her belly. Biba shivered with desire as his fingers found the waistband of her jeans.

When he slid her jeans from her legs, she felt the familiar terror that came with any intimacy, but she fought it. She wanted this man so badly, wanted him so entirely. His fingers were at the sides of her panties now, and he drew them gently down her legs.

In such a vulnerable position, completely naked with the man who held all the power, Biba felt both a terror and a desperation for his touch she might explode. She reigned it in, wanting to undress Cosimo as tenderly as he had her.

When she freed his cock, thick and long, from his underwear, she felt it pulse and stiffen in her hand; she knew this was right and had never been so sure of anything in her life. Cosimo kissed her, his eyes never leaving her face. "Are you sure?"

Biba nodded, knowing she could not hide her nervousness from him. "Do you have a...?"

Cosimo smiled and grabbed his jeans, pulling a condom out of the back pocket. "Don't think badly of me...I just wanted to be prepared."

That he had been thinking of making love to her made her stomach warm. Cosimo slid his hand between her legs and began to stroke her.

Instantly, her body reacted as if it were being attacked. No, stop it, Biba told her subconscious fiercely. I want this man. Do not ruin it for me.

She forced herself to focus only on Cosimo's beautiful face, the softness of his lips against hers. She wrapped her legs around his waist and felt his cock nudge at her sex.

"I want you," she whispered, and Cosimo nodded.

"My darling Biba..."

It wasn't Cosimo's fault, of course, and she wanted him so badly she could scream. She focused on his kisses, so sweet, so loving. She shivered through the pleasure of him kissing her, but something in her brain was stopping her from reaching the heights she had imagined. When she felt his cock notch into her entrance, her body panicked and bucked. "No, please stop... please...I'm sorry." She burst into tears.

Cosimo held her as she recovered, studying her face. "Sweet Biba...are you okay?"

Tell him. "No... Cosimo, it would be my...first time."

His expression went from aroused to shocked, and he sat up. "Your first time?"

She nodded, suddenly feeling miserable. "I'm sorry."

Cosimo ran his hands through his hair, sitting back on his haunches. He was magnificent to look at: hard-bodied, his cock still half-erect, a fine sheen of sweat on his olive skin despite the cool of the lake's mist. Biba sat up, feeling exposed, and Cosimo seemed to notice, pulling his sweater around her naked body and settling down next to her, wrapping her in his arms. "Please, there's no need for you ever to apologize...I just feel like I've let you down. If I had known..."

"I wanted you," Biba said firmly. "I still want you. But something inside me is...broken."

Cosimo frowned. "Being a virgin isn't being broken, lovely one." He searched her eyes, and she saw understanding creep into them. "Oh, God...Biba..."

She nodded. "A family friend when I was twelve. Not rape, but there was other stuff. So, I waited until I knew I really wanted someone. And I met you."

"Dear God. I want to kill him." He pressed his lips against her forehead. "How did your parents react?"

Her throat closed, and she leaned into his embrace. "They didn't believe me."

"Jesus Christ." He spat the words, clearly incensed, and his arms tightened around her. "Darling, I wish you had said something before."

She looked up at him. "Would you still want me if I had?"

His green eyes were troubled. "We should have talked about it... God, Biba. I'm old enough to be your father."

"Don't say that, Cosimo. I've never felt like this before." Biba kissed him, but she could feel him holding back now. God... "Please don't push me away."

Cosimo's brows were knitted together. "That's not what I'm doing." He began to pull her clothes onto her, and eventually, they both dressed.

Biba felt miserable as they walked back down the jetty. Cosimo took her hand. "Biba, we're going to go back to my room, and we're going to talk. Okay?"

She nodded, but knew in her heart, he was about to tell her that they couldn't continue. She felt like crying. She wanted him so badly, but it was just her screwed-up brain that was putting the skids on this.

That, and the fact that this man couldn't possibly want a messed-up kid with no experience and one hell of a damaged past. *Please don't send me away...*

Biba was about to stop him and beg him not to leave her, but then a scream pierced the night, and shots rang out. Looking at each other in horror, Cosimo and Biba only hesitated a moment before both of them took off, running towards the sound of the gunfire.

## CHAPTER SEVEN

Stella was hyperventilating as Gunter tried to comfort her. "Someone tried to take me," she wailed as she saw Cosimo and Biba arrive.

"We heard gunfire," Cosimo said, looking at Gunter, who nodded.

"It was Rich. He took off chasing the guy."

Stella, sniffing, and obviously genuinely scared, left Gunter's arms and went to Cosimo. Cosimo had no choice but to put his arms around the distressed woman. "It's okay. You're okay."

Rich came back then, sweating, his eyes darting everywhere. "Guy got away, I'm sorry. Stella, you okay?"

Stella, happy in Cosimo's arms, nodded. "It was just scary. How did he get in?"

"Well, unfortunately, it's pretty open here, and the studio won't pay for total protection," Rich was breathless. "It's difficult to police with just us." He looked at Cosimo. "Sorry, boss."

"Not your fault. Listen, hire some more guys. I'll pay for it. Stella, do you feel safe in your room?"

She shook her head. "Maybe I should move closer to your room, Cosimo."

Biba felt a flash of jealousy run through her, especially when Cosimo nodded. "We'll get you a suite in the big house. Biba can stay with you, then we can protect you both."

Stella didn't look enthusiastic, and Biba agreed with her. Sharing a suite would mean neither could indulge in secret assignations…was Cosimo doing it on purpose?

Biba trailed behind them as they walked up to the manor. She felt miserable and guilty. Miserable because she had blown it spectacularly with Cosimo, and guilty because clearly, Stella had been in danger. What the hell was going on?

Rich caught up with her. "You okay, boo?" She nodded but felt even more guilty. She'd said yes to a date with Rich and not even an hour later, she was naked with their boss. God, she was a mess, wasn't she? Maybe Cosimo was right. Maybe the incident with Damon had fucked her up more than she liked to admit.

SHE GOT the answer to one question a little later when she and Stella were alone. They were changing for bed: Stella walking around completely naked, Biba shimmying into her shorts and T-shirt discreetly as always. She felt Stella watching her.

"Were you and Cosimo together earlier?" Stella was smoking a cigarette, blowing the smoke out of the window. "You seemed to arrive at my trailer at the same time."

Ah. So, Stella had been watching them. "I was down by the lake at the same time, is all," Biba said casually. "We just said hello when we heard the gunshots." She was amazed at how easily the lie slid from her lips, but she really didn't want to deal with Stella's jealousy tonight.

"Huh." Stella was fishing, Biba could tell. "I didn't know you two were on chatting terms."

"He was being polite."

Stella seemed satisfied with that, but an hour later, Stella snoring gently beside her, Biba couldn't help reliving the soft kisses, the taste of his skin, the way his intense gaze made her stomach flutter with desire. With it though, came a sense of certainty, of misery, knowing that by the way Cosimo reacted, there would be no repeat of this evening's intimacy.

He's right to withdraw, she thought, but the idea of being distant with him now was making her chest hurt.

She finally fell into a fitful sleep, only to be woken by Stella a couple of hours later, showing her the note that had been sent to her.

My darling Stella,

Know that tonight was just the beginning. We will together soon, my love, and you will never have to worry about anything ever again. If anyone tries to stop our love, know that I will do anything to stop them. Anything. Your director, the security teams, that pretty assistant of yours...all of their lives will be forfeit if they try to stop me.

Soon, my darling.

Soon.

Cosimo had called in the FBI, and they had agreed. "Guy's a nutball," Luke Harris, the FBI agent, said with a nod to them as they all gathered in the manor's dining hall. "Luckily for you, nutballs are our thing."

Biba hid a smirk at the agent's words, shooting a look at Reggie. She knew he was thinking the same thing—this dude was a swaggering moron. Still, this wasn't about their opinions, rather Stella's safety. Biba didn't even register that she too had been threatened until Cosimo spoke up. "Agent Harris, I need reassurances that Stella, Biba, and the rest of our staff are safe."

"We'll do what we can, but I have to say, with respect to Mr. Furlough and Mr. Wolff, your security here is lax. That this guy could break in and return later to leave a note…"

"Maybe he left the note before he tried to take Stella." Biba spoke up, wanting to defend Cosimo. "It would make more sense."

Harris looked miffed. "I don't see…"

"It would make more sense. After all, he threatened to take Stella, and then tried to do exactly that. Perhaps Stella didn't get the note before because it was at the manor's reception?" Cosimo's voice was smooth, but Biba detected anger in his tone. She was grateful for the backup.

Harris cleared his throat, two spots of pink appearing high on his cheeks. "We'll check it out. But what I said about the security stands. You need to beef it up."

"Already in motion," Cosimo shot a look at Rich who nodded.

"We have ten more security guards, and the manor house has offered to close down completely to outside people."

"It's a start." Harris looked back at Biba and Stella. "Be vigilant, little ladies. Don't go anywhere on your own."

Biba's eyes narrowed, and Stella looked angry. "Such good advice, Agent Harris. Our tax dollars well spent."

The sarcasm went over his head, and he left shortly after. "You asked for miracles, Theo. I give you the F.B.I.," Reggie drawled in his best Alan Rickman/Die Hard impression.

It broke the tension—even Cosimo grinned. "Hey, listen…I'm sorry, folks. I've dealt with a lot of weirdos in my time, but I promise, I'll do everything I can to protect you." He sighed, rubbing his eyes. He looked tired and drawn, and Biba wanted more than anything to hold him, kiss him, tell him everything would be fine.

FOR THE REST of the day, however, he kept his distance. They had all agreed that working would be best for them all to decompress and distract themselves from the unpleasantness of Stella's stalker. Stella, of course, was milking it for all it was worth, but when she was acting, Biba had to give it to her, it lent a certain vulnerability to her character which made her more likable.

However diva-like and bitchy Stella could be, the one thing Biba loved about her was her performances. There was a reason Stella Reckless was the biggest movie star in the world: sheer magnetism and radiance. She was luminescent in front of the camera. Stella loved acting even more than she loved herself, and it showed. When she wasn't causing trouble for the sake of it, she could deliver searing, hypnotizing performances which were peerless. Today was a day like that, and Biba watched Franco, her costar in today's scenes, rise to the challenge. Despite the vast age difference, they were magnetic together, the romance between them utterly believable.

During the afternoon, Damon's replacement, Sifrido, arrived on set and had an immediate impact on the cast and crew. Friendly, flirty, easy-going, Sifrido and Franco bonded straight away, and Biba could tell they would have fun teasing Stella. For her part, Stella didn't seem to mind—she loved the extra attention.

Sifrido also had an effect on Cosimo. Biba could tell they were old friends with their easy joking around and the way Cosimo's tension level seemed to ease. She was glad...although he still wasn't meeting her gaze.

Let it go. Give him time. But it still hurt. Biba distracted herself with work and talking to Rich and Gunter. Rich was quieter than usual and later, when she asked him if he was okay, he pulled her aside. "Beebs...I can't leave this unsaid, but I saw you. You and Cos, down by the lake."

Her face flaming, Biba groaned. "God, Rich, I'm so sorry. That was...it wasn't planned, I swear. And, in the end, nothing happened. It was a moment of...madness. I'm sorry."

"You don't owe me an apology," Rich said with a smile, "or anything else. I can relate. We've all had that moment. I just didn't want to know that and have you not know. It's okay, really."

Biba looked at him. "I do like you, Rich, a lot. This thing with Cosimo...I couldn't help myself, and maybe that tells me something."

"I gotcha. Hell, listen, as long as we're friends..."

"Always, Rich. Always."

Rich grinned, nudging her shoulder. "And if you like him, you should go for it. Cos is a good guy."

"I don't think there will be a repeat of what happened between us, but thanks."

BIBA WAS BACK in Stella's trailer even before Stella finished work for the day, and when her boss got back, she gave Biba a strange look. Biba looked up from her laptop. "Oh, sorry, was I meant to bring you something?"

"No, it's fine. It's just unlike you to hide away in here."

"Not hiding away, just catching up on e-mails."

"Even so." Stella sat down opposite her, tapping out a cigarette from her pack. "Cosimo asked where you'd gone."

Biba hid the thrill that went through her. "Oh?"

"Said he wanted to talk security with you."

"Okay. I should go find him." She got up, trying not to run right out of the trailer and go find him. She went through the mail and handed it to Stella. "No nasties, but nothing much of interest either."

Stella threw the stack on the table. "I'll get to it. So, you and Cosimo seem to be connecting."

"Just as colleagues." Biba hated lying but there it was. "I better go find him; he may want to talk about your security detail."

"Okay." But there was an icy tone to Stella's voice—she didn't believe Biba's claims of simple friendship with Cosimo. Biba shrugged and left the trailer.

AT THE MANOR, she asked the receptionist where Cosimo was. "I think Mr. DeLuca is in his suite," the young man said with a smile. "Want me to call up?"

"Yes, please."

Biba waited patiently as he called Cosimo. A second later, he smiled at her. "He says to go up."

Heart pounding, she took the stairs to the second floor, needing the exercise to shed some nervous energy. Tapping lightly at Cosimo's door, she still jumped slightly when he opened it almost immediately.

For a long moment, they gazed at each other, then he smiled. "Hey."

"Hey yourself."

"Come on in."

He stood back to let her in, and as she passed, she smelled soap and shampoo, saw his dark curls were damp, his sweater freshly on. Her senses reeled, and she wobbled.

"Hey, are you alright?" Cosimo caught her before she fell. Biba, mortified, nodded. "Sorry, I forgot to eat today."

He rolled his eyes and grinned at her. "Now, I already know that's not like you."

God, why did his smile make her stomach hurt? Cosimo called down and ordered room service for them both. "Little impromptu dinner party."

Biba chuckled. "Can it really be a party with just two?"

Cosimo considered. "Okay, a suite picnic."

"Nice."

Cosimo laughed. "Burgers okay with you? I ordered all the fixings."

"Perfect. I just forgot to eat today."

Cosimo sat down next to her, and she leaned against him. He put his arm around her. "Biba..."

"I know what you're going to say. I'm too young; I'm still a virgin; I'm damaged from my past; You can't take on someone with so much baggage."

Cosimo gave her a sad smile. "The first three are true. The last, not so much. Except...I can't take advantage of you. I would never be able to forgive myself if I caused you more pain."

Biba nodded, misery seeping through every cell in her body. "I know. It's the responsible thing to do."

He pressed his lips to her temple. "It's not that I don't want you, Biba, because, Lord knows, I do. But I have a responsibility towards you, the movie, and my son, of course."

Biba looked up at him—he was so Goddamn beautiful she could cry. "I know. Nicco comes first. And hey, on the bright side, if we stop this before it begins, we have a good shot at being friends."

She saw him visibly relax. "I think so, too. There's nothing I'd like more...well, there's one thing, but that's not an option."

"Yet..." Biba said, her voice was almost a whisper, willing him to agree. He met her gaze steadily.

"Yet."

Their eyes locked, and then his lips were against hers. "God damn it," he said as they paused for air.

Biba chuckled. "Look, let's do this. When room service arrives, that's the holy line of demarcation. That's when we cross from whatever this is to just friends. Until then..."

He groaned and took her face in his hands, his lips hungry against hers. "I hope they forget our order."

"Me, too."

But room service came quickly and efficiently, and Cosimo and Biba broke apart regretfully. As they sat down with their burgers, Biba smiled at him. "Actually, once you see the wolverine way I eat fast food, you'll be put off me anyway."

Cosimo laughed. "Is that so?"

Biba took a huge bite of her burger, making a growling noise and chomping loudly. Cosimo laughed and followed suit until they were both laughing helplessly. Biba almost choked on her burger. "Told you so."

Cosimo reached over and wiped a smear of mustard from her bottom lip, making it tingle. "You weren't exaggerating."

"So, as an Italian American, are you big into pizza and stuff?"

"Actually, I'm just Italian. I was born in Venice."

Biba's eyebrows shot up. "Really? Well, dang that search engine."

"Ha. You Googled me?"

Biba rolled her eyes. "Of course I Googled you, dude. I'm a millennial."

Cosimo groaned again. "God, I feel old." Biba grinned.

"So, Mr. Italian, what's the food like over there?"

"Sublime. Haven't you been? I thought I heard your father was stationed in Europe for a while."

"Germany. And he wasn't big on vacations. Or being a father." She didn't know why she blurted that out, but Cosimo nodded.

"From what you told me last night, I wouldn't think so.

God…you believe your child." He spat the words out, and Biba was touched he was so angry on her behalf.

"You'd think. It took me a while to figure out that it wasn't normal family behavior to be like that, and that it wasn't my fault. He failed me. My mom failed me. And I have every right to be angry about it."

"If I could go back and kill the guy who did this to you, I wouldn't hesitate." His green eyes were almost dangerous-looking now, and a shiver went down Biba's spine. She could believe it.

"Thank you." She wanted to change the subject now. "You must be looking forward to seeing Nicco next weekend?"

Cosimo nodded, then sighed. "Yes and no. I have a feeling that it'll be twenty-four hours of monosyllabic conversation and heavy teenage sighs."

"He is sixteen."

"Yeah. Look, this may be asking a huge favor but…"

"I'd love to," she said preempting his question. "I can think up some cool stuff he might enjoy…I could bring Reggie, too. He always seems to know the places to be in the city."

Cosimo looked relieved. "I'd be very grateful. I just can't reach him at the moment."

Biba nodded, and for a few minutes they ate in companionable silence. "Can I be personal for a moment?"

Cosimo nodded. "Of course."

"Stop thinking you're old. You carry this world-weary look around with you—but look at you. You're only forty, and you look fifteen years younger than that when you smile. I know losing your wife must have been the worst, the absolute worst. But she would want you to be happy, Cos."

Biba blushed scarlet after her little speech. Who was she to lecture this grown-up? But he smiled at her. "You're good at this friend thing."

"I try."

Cosimo reached over and linked his fingers with hers. Biba could barely stand the tension between them and slowly withdrew her hand. "I can't."

"I know, I'm sorry."

They finished their meal and Biba stood. "I had better go tell Stella that we just talked."

"We did just talk."

"True." She smiled at him as he walked her to the door. "Thank you for dinner."

He opened the door for her, but then shut it again before she could leave, closing his eyes. "Biba…"

She pressed her lips to his. "I know."

They kissed again slowly, and then held each other for a long moment. "Bye, buddy," she said, softly, trying to make him smile, but he shook his head.

"If you only knew what I was thinking."

She touched his face. "I really do know. Goodnight, Cosimo."

"Goodnight, Biba."


IT WAS ONLY when she knew she was truly alone that Biba let herself cry.

# CHAPTER EIGHT

"Nicco will be here tomorrow morning," Cosimo told her a week later. "He's coming down on the bus. I said I'd send a car for him."

"He's just showing his independence. Let him."

"Yes, oh wise one."

Biba chuckled, nudging him gently in the ribs as they stood in the craft services line. Cosimo wasn't one of those directors who demanded to be served first. When they had their meal, they sat down with Rich and Gunter. Gunter was in the middle of one of his rants.

"But why zey exist at all? Zey are just demons disguised as fluffy bees but without ze fluff. Zey are the devils."

Rich looked bemused. Biba grinned at him. "What's he talking about?"

"Wasps. Damn wasps."

"Demons."

"They're just wasps, dude."

Gunter grumbled to himself, and Cosimo grinned. "You have a strange relationship with the insect world, Gunter."

"I just don't know how zey make a life."

Biba scooped a spoonful of granola into her mouth. "Cosimo's son is coming to Tacoma tomorrow."

"Cool. What are you going to do?"

Cosimo smiled. "Biba's in charge of the day's activities. I like to call it 'The How-to-Amuse-a-Teen Challenge.'"

"I got you covered, Cos," Biba said, marveling at how easily they could be 'just friends' in front of everyone else. When they had been alone this past week, they'd struggled not to break their new rule. More than a few kisses had sneaked through their 'holy line of demarcation'. "Nicco is going to be so impressed; he'll tell all his friends what a cool dad he has."

Cosimo snorted. "When hell freezes over maybe."

"Cosimo?" Stella appeared, glancing at Biba with a very frosty look. Biba crunched her granola and ignored her. "Can I borrow you for a sec?"

"Sure."

Cosimo followed Stella away from the group. Stella turned to face him. "What are you doing with Biba?"

"Excuse me?"

"The late-night talks, the hanging out. She's twenty-one years old and impressionable. I worry that she has a crush on you."

God, I hope so. "Don't be ridiculous, Stella. She's my employee. I'm making sure that she is okay after the attack and that the studio's liability isn't put in jeopardy. Biba could sue us for what happened."

Stella snorted. "She wouldn't do that. I know her. She'll forget it easily enough."

"How well do you actually know Biba?" Cosimo was curious.

"Well enough. Leave her alone, Cosimo. Look for someone your own age."

Cosimo's sense of humor failed him then. "Stella, for one thing, my friendship with Biba is not your business. Secondly, don't lecture me on appropriateness when you brought Damon Tracy to this set."

He stalked off towards the manor, feeling more guilty than angry now. The truth was…he was falling for Biba, and he wasn't doing a whole lot to stop himself. He meant what he said to Stella—it was none of her business—and at least her suspicions had stopped her over-the-top seduction routines. She'd gotten the message; he wasn't interested in her. Cosimo hoped she wouldn't take her disappointment out on Biba, but he knew that was a very real possibility.

He went to his suite and stripped off, going into the bathroom and cranking on the shower. He had to get over this thing with Biba. For her part—save for the odd kiss—she had resolutely stuck to their agreement, and he was grateful that it hadn't affected their friendship.

Tomorrow, she would meet his son, a boy she was so much closer to in age and experience that Cosimo wondered if it would make a difference in his feelings for her. He didn't think so.

He couldn't stop thinking about her, her soft lips, those big brown eyes, that caramel skin. When they had been naked together, just holding her had been so thrilling. God, he wanted to make love to her.

Maybe in a couple of years, maybe…but he knew he was in trouble. Biba had gotten under his skin in a way no one ever had —not even Grace.

He was going through his notes for the next week's filming when there was a knock at the door. He opened it to find his old friend Sifrido grinning at him. "Sorry that I'm not a certain little cutie-pie?"

Cosimo laughed. Sifrido knew him well. "Is it that obvious?"

"Only to those who know you well. Can I come in?"

"Of course. Mini-fridge is full if you want a beer."

"Hit me."

Cosimo snagged two beers from the fridge and handed one to Sifrido. "So, you need to catch me up on your life. What's it been, two years?"

"Five and don't change the subject. What gives between you and the lovely Biba?"

Cosimo sighed, his shoulders slumping. "I'll sound like a creep."

"Not possible, buddy."

Cosimo grinned. "You sound more American every day."

"You're prevaricating." Cosimo had forgotten that Sifrido was a no-nonsense kind of guy.

Cosimo shrugged. "I'm crazy about her. She's like a blast of cool, clean air. She's funny, smart, and doesn't take any shit."

"And she's beautiful."

"That's incidental."

Sifrido raised his eyebrows but didn't call Cosimo on his statement. "Is she okay after what Damon did to her?"

Cosimo hesitated. "I can't answer that for sure. 'Frido, what I'm about to tell you can't leave this room."

"You have my word."

"We almost made love the other evening. Out on the jetty on the lake."

Sifrido looked impressed. "Almost?"

"She stopped it, and of course, I was okay with that. She told me she was...conflicted. Something happened to her when she was a kid."

"She's a virgin?"

Cosimo nodded, feeling disloyal to Biba, but he had to talk things through with someone. "The abuse didn't progress to rape, not that it's any less horrific. So...I can't pursue anything with her. It wouldn't be fair."

"To you or her?" Sifrido took a swig of his beer. "Don't you think you putting the skids on a relationship you both wanted would make her feel even worse? My sister got raped at twenty-four. You know Clara. She didn't let it stop her falling in love. She knew the difference between rape and sex. One is violence. The other comes from a place of love. You want to help Biba? Love her. Trust yourself. Trust her to learn—if she doesn't already know—the difference. She seems like a smart girl."

Cosimo felt his heart lift a little. He leaned forward. "There's also the fact I'm her boss."

"So? How long will you be filming here?"

"Another six weeks."

"That's nothing. If you want her, but are afraid of lawsuits, wait six weeks. See how you both feel then. You deserve love, my old friend."

"Old is right."

"Bullshit. You're still young."

When Sifrido had said goodnight, Cosimo went to bed but lay awake thinking about Biba. He closed his eyes and imagined running his hand slowly down her body, cupping the full breasts, stroking the soft curve of her belly. He imagined taking her clit into his mouth, teasing and licking at the small bud until she was gasping and so wet for him that sliding his big cock into her would be easy—pain-free for her and totally exhilarating for both of them.

Cosimo groaned and rolled out of bed, heading to the bathroom where he masturbated slowly, thinking about her, until he was shaking and groaning, his orgasm taking him over completely. "Biba," he whispered, leaning his hot forehead against the cool tile. Yep, he was in deep trouble.

When he went to bed, he dreamed of her, but it wasn't

pleasant dreams of lovemaking, but nightmares about someone stalking her, hurting her, taking her away from him.

At four a.m. Cosimo woke, shivering and sweating. He got out of bed and poured himself a Scotch, draining it in one go.

He couldn't bring himself to go back to sleep that night, not wanting to see any more horrifying visions of the woman he was falling in love with, bleeding out and dying in his arms.

## CHAPTER NINE

The nightmares were blown away the next morning by Biba's cheerful smile at the craft service trailer. "Hey, dude. Today's the day?"

For a moment, Cosimo was confused. "Huh?"

Biba pretended to knock on his head. "Your son, remember?"

God, Nicco, of course. He grinned at her. "I'm glad you're cheerful about today, because I guarantee Nicco won't be."

"If he hated the idea that much, he wouldn't have come."

"There's still time for him to cancel."

Biba grinned at his woebegone face. "Is that so? So that handsome young boy over there isn't your son then?"

Cosimo turned in surprise to see Nicco, taller than ever, stalking towards him. He stepped forward to hug his son, which Nicco accepted to Cosimo's surprise. He stepped back and studied his son.

Nicco had always looked more like Grace than Cosimo: he had Grace's Korean coloring, straight jet-black hair teased up into spikes, and dark brown, almost black eyes. Only his build and his height seemed to come from Cosimo.

Cosimo stepped away and introduced his son to Biba, who

held out her fist for a bump. Nicco's eyes lit up when he saw her, and Cosimo hid a smile. Like father, like son—completely unable to resist Biba May's charms.

Cosimo drove Nicco, Biba, and Reggie into the city, and to Bob's Java Jive coffee house on South Tacoma Way. Biba sat up front with him; Nicco chivalrously opened the door for her. Apparently though, that was the extent of his engagement. Biba and Reggie both tried to start a conversation with the teen, and although he was polite, he quickly shut down any talk they might have shared.

Cosimo shot Biba a look as she tried again, and she winked at him. She wasn't going to give up on Nicco, and it warmed Cosimo's heart.

At the coffee house, which was shaped like a giant coffee pot, Biba got out. "Uh-oh…my bad. I don't think it opens until later. Hey, excuse me, sir?"

Cosimo watched her walk up to a man who was washing the outside windows of the place and converse with him for a few minutes. Working her magic again, she came back to them. "He says he can only do filter coffee at this hour, but he'll let us in as a favor."

As Reggie and Nicco got out of the car, Cosimo took her arm. "You are amazing," he murmured, and she beamed at him.

"I shamelessly dropped your name. It worked."

Cosimo laughed and reluctantly let go of her arm. He wanted to hold her hand, but it would be inappropriate, especially in front of Nicco.

As they sat in the coffeehouse chatting, Nicco seemed to thaw a little—a very little—but still looked bored. Biba nudged him with her elbow. "Come on, dude. This place is awesome."

Nicco nodded reluctantly. "It's okay."

"Man, you are hard work, you know that?" Biba grinned at him to soften the judgment. "You're such a teenager."

That got him. "Dude, you're like five seconds older than me."

"Try five years. You know what happened to me when I was sixteen? I learned the art of conversation." She crossed her eyes at him, making a face, and Nicco chuckled.

The sound of his son laughing made Cosimo's heart hurt. He hadn't heard that sound in years. "So," he said carefully, not wanting to break the mood, "where have our tour guides planned for next?"

"Well," Biba said, "we assumed that you and your friends have done pretty much everything in Seattle, so Reg and I researched some places to go. Fall City, for starters. Treehouses, dude."

Nicco nodded. "Grandma took me there last year."

Biba's face fell. "Really? Dang, I was looking forward to that."

Cosimo grinned at her sulky face. "I'm sure Nicco wouldn't mind going again."

"No, it's okay. I can go another time. Um...Reg?" Biba looked at her friend helplessly. She'd clearly set her heart on the treehouse. Cosimo told himself he would take her there one day.

"It's a drive, but we could go to the Observatory at Goldendale."

Nicco shrugged.

"Space not your nerd thing? Okay." Reggie was flicking through his phone. "We could catch a sea plane up to Friday Harbor?"

"Done it."

Cosimo shot a warning glance at his son, who ignored him.

"Look, it's okay," Nicco said. "We can just hang out at a mall or something."

"Thrilling," Cosimo said dryly, and Nicco flushed. He slid out of his chair.

"Gotta go pee."

Cosimo sighed and looked apologetically at Biba and Reggie. "I'm sorry, folks. I told you he was hard to entertain."

"I have a backup plan," Biba said, and both men looked at her. She grinned. "Do you trust me?" She addressed this to Cosimo, who nodded.

"With my life. Why?"

She sniggered to herself. "Because I'm about to say something to your sixteen-year-old son that might seem shocking... but just trust me. I think it may break the ice."

Cosimo looked at Reggie who nodded. "Okay. The floor is yours."

Still, when Biba said to Nicco on his return the words, "Right, Nic, we're going somewhere that celebrates blow jobs," Cosimo choked on his coffee, and Reggie put his head in his hands.

Nicco, though, perked up. "Really?"

"Really."

BIBA DROVE them this time to Dock Street, and they all got out of the car. Nicco looked around. "I don't get it."

Biba tugged him along. "Come on." They followed her over a bridge towards a cone-shaped building on the other side. Cosimo assumed that was where they were headed, but then halfway across, Biba stopped.

"Ta-dah! Nicco DeLuca, I present to you: a celebration of blow jobs." She indicated the wall in front of them, and Nicco began to laugh.

"Oh, very clever."

It was a wall with individual showcases of spectacularly blown glass sculptures. Cosimo was both relieved and grateful that now Nicco was laughing. He saw his son relax.

"You are a nutjob, you know that?" Nicco was saying to Biba now. She slung her arm around his shoulders.

"That'll teach you to be all teenage on us. Come on, you can actually walk under some of these lovelies, too."

All four of them strolled along the bridge underneath the glass ceiling. Cosimo and Reggie watched Biba and Nicco joke around with each other.

"She's amazing," Cosimo said, trying to keep most of his adoration out of his voice. Reggie nodded.

"She is that. Listen, I know you two have become friends. Maybe you could help me out with something."

"Sure."

"It's Biba's birthday in a week. I haven't any idea what to do for it other than a party, but that seems lame. Also, Biba's not wild about them. Maybe we could do something at the manor, out on the lake. Fireworks, maybe?"

Cosimo nodded. "Sounds perfect. I'll set it up." Realizing then that he was talking to Biba's best friend and maybe he, Cosimo, was overstepping, stopped. "I mean, if you want me to, Reg. Biba's your person."

Reggie grinned. "It's okay, I know what you mean, and I'd like your help. That's why I asked. You think Stella would be okay with it?"

"I really don't care if she isn't," Cosimo said, "it's Biba's birthday. I mean," he said, shaking his head in disbelief as he saw Nicco and Biba play-fight, "look what she's doing for me."

LATER, as Reggie and Nicco were trying glass-blowing for themselves, Cosimo took Biba aside. "I can't thank you enough for today. Blow jobs?"

Biba snickered, beaming up at him. "And I had a backup to

my backup plan...the Afterglow Vista in Friday Harbor, the Mima Mounds in Olympia."

Cosima was laughing. "Stop."

"The Junk Castle in..." Biba was cut off as Cosimo kissed her, pouring every ounce of desire into it. Her fingers slid into his hair as he took her in his arms. Luckily, they were behind a stack of glass, away from the others.

Biba was the one to pull away. "I'm sorry."

"I started the kiss. Don't apologize." He leaned his forehead against hers. "God, Biba, I know what I said, but I want you so badly."

"Me, too," she whispered. She hesitated then slid her hand down to his groin. Cosimo's cock responded immediately, thickening and throbbing against his jeans as she stroked the mound of it. "Cosimo...I want it to be you. I want it to be you so badly..."

He kissed her again, feeling her tremble in his arms. "We can make this work, can't we? Us?"

"Not trying is killing me," she admitted, her voice low and gravelly. "Every time I'm near you, I just want to touch you and have your hands on my body...and you inside me. I'm scared, yes, but I want you so badly."

They kissed again, then heard voices approaching. They broke apart but shared a long look. Both of them relaxed, knowing now that they would be together—that it was inevitable.

Nicco had truly relaxed now, and as they went for food at the Southern Kitchen on Sixth Avenue, he even talked about school and what he had planned for his future.

"College," said Cosimo firmly, and Nicco grinned.

"Don't worry, Pa. It's on my list."

"Subject?" Biba was stuffing fried chicken and gravy into her mouth.

Nicco smiled. "Bathymetry."

"Ah," Biba said, "You like the ocean?"

Nicco looked surprised. "You know what bathymetry is?"

Biba grinned. "Just because I went on a click-a-link fest on Wikipedia once. I'm obsessed with volcanoes."

Cosimo looked surprised, and Reggie chuckled. "Yeah, she'll do that. Random stuff. She's a space nerd, too."

"True story. So, you want to work for...?" She addressed the question back to Nicco.

"NOAA. And I want to study underwater volcanoes." He laughed, bemused to find a kindred spirit amongst his dad's friends. He shot his father an admiring look, and Cosimo knew he had won major points for having Biba on his team. More reason to be grateful to her.

"Have you been up Mount Rainier?" Biba had finished her fries and was now stealing them from Nicco's plate.

Nicco shook his head. "Never got around to it."

"Why don't you and your dad go tomorrow? Before you go back to Seattle?"

Clever Biba. He squeezed her leg under the table and nodded at Nicco. "You want to?"

"Yeah, that sounds cool."

Cosimo didn't know whether to laugh or cry. His son thought hanging out with him was cool? He felt his throat close with emotion. Biba glanced at him, feeling his body tense beside her. Sliding her hand under the table, she entwined her fingers with his and squeezed them.

That was the moment Cosimo DeLuca fell in love with Biba May.

## CHAPTER TEN

Biba had fallen asleep in the car on the way back to Lakewood Manor, and when they reached the place, Cosimo felt like he couldn't offer to help her back to her room. He had Nicco to consider and besides, she was more than capable of finding her own way to her room. She hugged Nicco hard. "Have a great day tomorrow with your dad, okay?"

"I will...and thanks for today."

She hugged Cosimo a little harder. "Enjoy tomorrow. Progress had been made," she whispered in his ear, and because it was the one facing away from the others, she kissed his neck quickly. "Goodnight, folks. Come on, Reginald, you look more shattered than I am."

She bore Reggie off along the hallway, and Cosimo let Nicco into the suite. "You can take the bed. I'll use the pull-out."

Nicco hesitated. "Dad, have you...in that bed?"

"Have I what?" Cosimo took a minute to get what his son was talking about. "Dude, no. You're good."

"Well, I don't know what goes on, like, on a film set. I hear things." Nicco snickered at his father's eye roll.

"If you knew how uneventful life on a film set really was."

Cosimo was grabbing a pillow from the bed and a blanket from the closet.

"Maybe I could come down, hang out, see what happens one day?"

Cosimo stopped, but then realized he shouldn't make a big deal of what Nicco had said. "Anytime, pal, you know that."

"Cool. Night, Dad."

When Nicco had gone to bed, Cosimo stripped down to his underwear and turned off the light. He saw his phone blinking with a message. Laying down on the pull-out bed, he grabbed his phone and scrolled through to the message. Biba.

Progress, progress, progress! I think we broke though the teenage barrier! B xx

Cosimo chuckled softly. All thanks to you, my lovely Biba. I can't thank you enough. C xx

There were few moments before she replied and when he read it, his heart began to beat faster.

Show me. Tomorrow night. Show me.

And that was all she needed to say.

## CHAPTER ELEVEN

Biba jiggled her legs under the dinner table so much that Reggie actually held her knees down. "Why are you so hyped up?"

Biba felt her face redden. Because tonight, I'm going to have sex for the first time with the man of my dreams. "Nothing, just excess energy. Good day yesterday, huh?"

"Very. Nicco's a good kid. Can't see any of Cosimo in him, can you?"

Biba thought about it. "Didn't notice. He's fun when you break the ice. That's like Cosimo."

Reggie studied her, his brown eyes searching her face. "You like him."

"Who, Nicco?"

"No, Cosimo. Think I didn't notice the chemistry between you?"

Biba said nothing, but she could feel her face burning. Reggie nudged her, lowering his voice. "Go for it, Beebs. He's obviously into you."

Not yet, but later tonight... God, she had to talk about it to someone. "Come with me."

They walked down to the lake and sat on the same jetty where Biba and Cosimo had almost made love. She told Reggie about that night. He grinned widely. "I knew something was up with you. But you didn't go through with it?"

She shook her head. "No, my big dumb brain stopped it. And when I told Cosimo why, he kind of backed off. Not that he wasn't kind."

"Well, now, that's admirable. He did exactly the right thing."

"Except…"

"Except what?"

Biba flushed again—at this rate she'd be scarlet all day. "Tonight…"

Reggie looked surprised. "You're ready?"

Biba nodded. "I'm nervous, of course, but I really believe I can do this because I want to do it so badly. And I trust Cosimo, Reggie. You know how much of a big thing that is for me."

"I do, honey." Reggie hugged her. "I'm really happy for you, Beebs. This is one of those moments."

"It is."

They looked out over the lake in companionable silence for a few minutes, then Reggie tickled the back of her neck. "Beebs? Have you seen your mom and dad since we've been in Tacoma?"

She shook her head. "No."

"The base is less than a mile away."

"I know." She turned to look at him. "I have no feeling for them, Reg. No love, no hate, just nothing. They lost the right to call me daughter when they didn't believe me." Biba looked away again. "The bastard that abused me was later arrested for doing the same thing to three more children. Did you know that?"

Reggie shook his head, his eyes serious. "I didn't."

"My parents never called to apologize. Not once. They would

have known about the arrest, too. So, Reg, that tells me everything I need to know. End of subject."

"Fair enough." Reggie kissed her cheek. "Love you, bugs."

"Love you, too." She drew in a shaky breath. "God, why am I so nervous?"

"Because Cosimo means something to you," Reggie said fervently. "That's good. That's perfect. Don't worry, take it easy." He grinned at her. "Got some condoms?"

Biba looked alarmed. "God, no..."

"Relax, boo. This is a movie set. Makeup has a drawer full."

Biba grimaced. "I wish I didn't know that."

Reggie got up and pulled her to her feet. "Come on. Knowing Stella, she's looking for you. I'll get some condoms for you. Have a great night."

STELLA WAS in a very bad mood despite the fact they weren't working that day. "Look at all this mail," she moaned, heaving a stack onto the table. "I thought you were going to keep on top of it."

"I do my best, Stel."

"You could have thinned this out yesterday."

Biba gritted her teeth. "I don't work Saturdays, you know that."

Stella, having lit a cigarette, picked a bit of tobacco off of her tongue. "Maybe I should get an assistant who doesn't need days off."

"Good luck with that. Why are you in bitch mode?" As if Biba didn't know. Stella had obviously seen her come back from the day out with Cosimo and Nicco.

Stella didn't answer her question. She nodded at the mail. "Get to it then, I don't have all day."

Actually, you do. But Biba said nothing, instead swiftly sorting the mail into three piles: fan, work, junk. Stella scooped up the junk and threw it in the trash can. Biba retrieved it with a glare and put it in the recycling bin. Mini battles were what their relationship was based on.

Stella started to look through the work pile. "Crap. Crap. Crap. Ha! The Weinstein Company—no thanks." She dumped that one in the trash with a flourish.

Biba nodded. That was something they could agree on. She looked through the fan mail, weeding out anything that needed a reply or a signed autograph. The final envelope she chose was a heavy manila one. As she shook out the contents, she saw they were just photos, no note. She picked a few up, noting they were sticky with something. Gross. Please don't be semen, please don't be semen...but then she noticed it had a red color and a sweet smell. Corn syrup. The stuff they used for blood on movie sets. Yikes.

She looked through the photos, unease curling through her stomach. Mostly, they were pictures of Stella on set or walking back to the manor. Taken on a phone, obviously. Then there were the five other photos. Cosimo, Rich, Reggie, Gunter, and herself. These were the ones with the fake blood on. They were being threatened.

"What is that?" Stella reached for it, but Biba pushed her hand away.

"Don't touch. We need to get these to the FBI."

She looked up and saw the fear in Stella's eyes. "Is it him?"

"I think so. So, the less we handle them the better."

"Should we call Cosimo?"

Biba shook her head. "I'll go talk to Rich and Gunter—they'll know what to do. Cosimo is hiking Mt. Rainier with his son today."

Stella sat back, her hands clenching and unclenching. "Is he threatening me?"

"Not you. I think whoever he is, he thinks he's in love with you. This message is really for the rest of us—we get in the way and we're..." She drew an imaginary knife across her throat, and Stella blanched.

"This is actually serious, right? If he's threatening to kill my friends..."

Biba didn't show how touched she was by that statement—mostly because she wasn't sure Stella meant it. "Nothing's going to happen, Stel, I promise. I know kung fu."

"You do?"

"No," Biba grinned at her boss, trying to make her laugh. "But I'm scrappy." She got up to find a plastic bag to put the envelope in.

Stella didn't smile. "If anyone got hurt because of me..."

Biba sat down opposite her boss. "First of all, in the unlikely event any of us got hurt, it would be because of him, the crazy—not you. This is not your responsibility."

"Yes, but you are."

Biba had to look away then because tears did fill her eyes. Her damn parents had never said that to her and now her diva-boss Stella was saying it? How fucked up was that? "Don't worry about it, Stella, really. We'll get to the bottom of this."

She went to find Rich and Gunter, and they called in Lars and Channing, Cosimo's seconds-in-command, and they agreed with Biba. No one else was to touch the letter, and they'd call in the FBI the next day to come collect it. Rich and Gunter made plans to beef up security. "You better tell Reggie to watch out, too," Rich said to Biba as they walked back to the trailers. "If he's in the nutjob's sights..."

"I will."

Biba went to find her best friend and met him in the lobby of the manor. "Here," he said, and stuffed her pockets with condoms. Biba colored immediately.

"Thank you. Listen, Reg, come sit with me. I have something to tell you.

## CHAPTER TWELVE

Nicco stood at the junction of the trail. "Which way?"

Cosimo, only a little way behind his son, nodded towards the Emmons Moraine Trail. "If we go that way, we'll get to see the Emmons Glacier. Largest in the contiguous States."

"Cool."

Cosimo didn't mind this one-word appraisal now. He'd learned as they hiked alongside the White River for the last hour or so, that Nicco was merely economical with his words. When Cosimo asked him about something he cared about, however, his son was erudite and knowledgeable and passionate.

As they walked now, he looked at his son. "So, I guess movie making and bathymetry don't have a lot of crossover that we can bond about."

Nicco shrugged. "I don't know... documentaries are cool."

"Who's your favorite?"

"Werner Herzog or the Maysles. Did you ever see Grizzly Man?"

Cosimo nodded. "That one kept me up at night."

"I know, right? The part where he tells the mother never to let anyone else hear Timothy Treadwell's screams? Holy cow." Nicco shook his head. "But I kind of loved Treadwell for his optimism. His love for the bears outweighed his sense of risk. Backfired, of course, but it was there."

"Nic... are you really only sixteen?" Cosimo shook his head, grinning, and Nicco laughed.

"Guess I'm just passionate about what I love, too...like my old man."

Cosimo smiled at him. "Maybe one day, we could make a documentary together."

Nicco nodded. "I'd like that."

They walked on a little further until they reached the glacier. "Woah." Nicco said, blowing out his cheeks.

"It's something, alright." Cosimo gazed out over the vista, and the two men enjoyed the view in silence for a few minutes.

"Want to double back, do the rest of the Great Basin?"

"Sure thing."

They went back down the spur and onto the main pathway. "So," Nicco said, and Cosimo detected a note of curiosity in his tone. "Biba..."

"Yes?"

Nicco grinned at his father. "You like her."

"Didn't you?"

"Dude, have you seen her? Of course I liked her, but not in that way. She's so cool. I mean, you like like her."

Cosimo didn't know where this was heading, so he didn't answer. Nicco play-punched his shoulder. "Dad, seriously...you should go for it. I could see you two were into each other. Reggie thinks so, too."

"It's that obvious?"

"Yup." Nicco bent down to study a plant at the side of the path. "Huh. Anyway, yes. You and Biba."

Cosimo considered. "You know there's nineteen years age difference?"

"So? Who gives a shit? You were, what, seven years older than Mom? It's just numbers. What counts is the chemistry."

"Jesus, you are an old man inside."

Nicco grinned. "About some things. I still love fart gags."

"Who doesn't?"

"I know, right? Apparently, that's immature to some people."

"Killjoys." Cosimo chuckled. "Nic...can we talk about...your mom?"

Nicco stopped, a look of pain crossing his face. "It's not that I want to forget she ever existed, Dad...it's just I'm not ready to talk about her. I feel like...I let her down."

"I can tell you that you didn't until I'm blue in the face, but until you believe it..." Cosimo nodded. "Just know, whenever you're ready, I'm here."

ON THE CAR RIDE BACK, Nicco was quieter, but when Cosimo dropped him off at the bus station, Nicco hugged him fiercely. "Thanks, Dad. I mean it."

"No problem. Love you, bud."

"Love you, too, Dad. I'll call you in a couple of days."

"Cool." Cosimo said and grinned at his son. Nicco laughed and rolled his eyes.

"Go get some, Pa," he shot back as he climbed the steps of the bus, and Cosimo laughed.

As he watched Nicco's bus pull away, Cosimo suddenly felt nervous. He and Biba had not planned what they would do this evening, where to meet, where to... God, his whole body was on fire, thinking about making love to her.

Cosimo drove back slowly to Lakewood, trying to steady his nerves. Biba would need him to be confident tonight—the weight of responsibility bore down on him, but he was determined they go on this journey together. He was crazy about her...heck, screw that, he was in love with her, had been practically since he met her. The mad chemistry between them made this inevitable.

He parked his car and was deep in thought as he walked slowly to the manor. In his room, he saw a note pushed under his door. He smiled when he saw the single word written on it in Biba's sprawling cursive.

Tonight.

God, yes. He grabbed a quick shower then took out his phone and called her. "Hey."

"Hey you." Her voice was soft. "Are you back?"

"I am. Where are you?"

"Dealing with a Reckless meltdown. Nothing serious, thankfully. Did you and Nicco have a great time?"

Cosimo grinned. "Darling, why are we talking on the phone when we could be talking in person? Have you eaten?"

"Not yet."

"Well, I have a suggestion. Date night. Let's have dinner, watch a movie. A proper date. If you're anything like me, you're nervous as hell."

Biba gave a relieved laugh. "Word, dude." She hesitated. "Shall I come to your suite?"

"I could come get you."

She laughed. "I think I know the way. When...?"

"I don't see any reason to postpone any longer, do you?" His voice was gruff with emotion, and he heard her intake of breath.

"No. No, I don't. I'll see you in a minute."

"I can't wait."

Luckily, he thought, housekeeping had been there, there were fresh sheets on the bed, and the room was tidy. He lit some of the scented candles in the room and dimmed the lights. He felt like a teenager on prom night.

At her knock, he opened the door and smiled at her. Biba was wearing a midnight blue smock dress which clung to her curves but was comfortable enough to lounge around in. "You're beautiful," he said and drew her into the room. He could feel her trembling as he slid his arms around her waist.

Cosimo stroked her face. "How are you?"

Biba chuckled a little shakily. "Terrified, actually." Cosimo bent his head down to kiss her mouth. So sweet...

"Me, too. We can take things slowly, baby. Shall we order some food and get relaxed?"

She nodded and, taking her hand, he led her to the couch, handing her a menu. She looked through it, but he could see she was beginning to panic. "Hey, Biba, we don't have to do anything you're not ready for. We can just chill out and talk. I just want to spend time with you."

It was her turn to kiss him, shaking her head. "I want this so badly. I'm trying to just keep calm, but God, I want you so much. Gosh," she laughed, "you wouldn't believe the confusion in my head right now."

"I love you." Cosimo hadn't known he would say it until right then, and the change in the room was immediate. "I'm so in love with you, Biba May. You have brought me back to life, and I want to spend every waking moment with you—and every un-waking moment. And if you're never ready to make love, it's okay. I just want to be with you..."

He didn't get to finish his declaration because Biba threw herself into his arms, kissing him, her cheeks damp with tears. "I love you, too! God, so, so much, Cosimo. I think I have loved you from the first moment we saw each other. I want you so badly, in every way."

She pressed her body against his, and he felt her breasts

against his hard chest, her belly against his, her legs wrapping around his waist as he lifted her into his arms. "Touch me," she said, "touch me everywhere and anywhere...Cosimo...Cosimo..."

He carried her into the bedroom and laid her gently down on the bed. "Biba, if at any time you want to stop, just say stop."

In answer, Biba sat up and impatiently pulled the dress over her head. "I don't want anything to stop," she said, and Cosimo laughed.

"You got it, baby."

She reached for his fly, unzipping his jeans. He stopped her. "Uh-uh. To start, this is all about you. Lay back for me, gorgeous. Let me see that spectacular body of yours."

Biba did as he asked her, stretching her lithe body, the dim candlelight making her dark skin glow like gold. Cosimo shook his head. "You are perfect. Utterly perfect."

He tugged his sweater over his head but left his jeans on as he lay next to her on his side. He smoothed his palm over her curves, leaving his hand splayed on her belly. "Biba... you are intoxicating." He could feel her belly quivering with nerves and desire.

Her large brown eyes seemed even bigger. He smiled down at her. "Now, I'm going to kiss you on every inch of this perfect body, starting with your cherry red lips..." He pressed his against hers and kissed her thoroughly, his tongue caressing hers as his hand stroked her belly. He moved down to her throat, then her breasts. Freeing one from its lacy cup, he took the nipple into his mouth, flicking his tongue around it, and sucking deeply until her heard her moan. His hand slipped into her panties, and as she gasped, he began to stroke her gently, his fingers making her clit harden and pulse.

"Cosimo..." Her whisper was one of desire rather than fear now, and he felt her sex become wet for him. He took her other nipple into his mouth, making it as rock hard as the first and continued to stroke her, increasing the pressure until he heard her gasp, give a little cry and tense. Her cunt was soaking now, but Cosimo took his time, moving down her body, kissing her belly, rimming her deep navel with his tongue, feeling her writhe beneath him. He slid his forefinger deep into her cunt, curving it up to find the G-spot, as his lips trailed down her belly.

He drew her panties down her legs gently and pushed her legs apart. He looked up at her. She was gazing at him, breathless. "Don't be scared, my darling."

Cosimo kissed the soft flesh of her inner thighs, slowly, tantalizingly, before taking her clit into his mouth. Biba was panting for air as she tensed and came again and again as he pleasured her. "God...yes...yes...please don't stop, don't ever stop..."

Cosimo trailed his lips up her body to take her mouth again. "Biba..."

"I want you inside me," she whispered, her face damp with dewy sweat, "Please, Cosimo. Don't wait."

Cosimo smiled and quickly took his jeans and underwear off. He sat back on his haunches as he rolled a condom down his huge, throbbing cock. He hitched her legs around his waist.

He'd made her so wet that sliding gently into her was easy, and he was gratified that she smiled up at him. "We fit together," she said, marveling at how well their bodies moved as one. Cosimo was glad that she seemed to be lost in their lovemaking, but not scared or distressed—rather, she clung to him out of animal desire only.

"I love you, I love you," she said, and her back arched up, and she cried out in ecstasy. Cosimo gathered her to him as he too peaked, groaning and calling out her name.

They collapsed together, panting and damp with sweat, kissing. Cosimo brushed her damp hair away from her forehead. "Are you okay?"

"More than okay, Cosimo, more than okay. Thank you, thank you..." She kissed him, her lips fierce against his. Cosimo cradled her in his arms.

"Thank you for trusting me to do this with you." He stroked her body. "How do you feel? Really?"

"My body feels kind of like jelly," Biba laughed, "like all my limbs are liquified...it's a lovely feeling."

Cosimo grinned. "I feel it, too. Listen, excuse me for a moment. I have to go deal with..." He nodded down to his still half-erect cock. "They take all the romance out of lovemaking, these condoms." He kissed her and slid off the bed to go deal with the condom.

"Nothing could ruin the romance of this for me," he heard her say and then laugh.

"What?" He went back into the bedroom and saw her grinning at him.

Biba giggled. "I said that and then my stomach gave the biggest rumble."

"Then let's order some food. We have all night to do whatever we want."

OVER A DINNER of flame-grilled steaks and a fresh green salad, followed by a fresh fruit salad, he told her about his day with Nicco. "Biba, we would have never gotten this far without what you did for us yesterday. And you should know...you've enchanted not just DeLuca Senior. Nicco adores you." Cosimo leaned over to kiss her. "He told me to 'go for it'."

"He's a very intelligent, very wise young man," Biba said with a smile. "I'm glad you took his advice. So, you think it's a beginning, or more?"

"I'm going to go with 'a beginning'. He's not ready to accept it wasn't his fault his Mom died, and he wasn't there. But it's a start—some building blocks in our relationship. I was despairing I'd lost him...until you."

Biba put down her fork and went into his arms, perching on his lap. "We're good for each other, Cosimo DeLuca."

He gazed up at her with those magnetic green eyes, and Biba felt her belly quiver with desire. He was so beautiful...her lover. She could hardly believe it. Cosimo DeLuca was her lover...and he truly loved her. Not just lust, but actual grown-up proper love. She leaned her forehead against his. "Cosimo?"

"Yes, my love?"

She grinned. "Take me to bed and fuck me senseless all night."

And with a grin, he did just that.

Soon. They were distracted: by the photos, by their director fucking Biba. Good. It would save anyone else from being hurt when he took Stella away from them. And he knew exactly when to do it. Stella would be his by this time next week, and all his planning would have been worth it.

He could hardly wait.

## CHAPTER THIRTEEN

Biba drifted back into consciousness, feeling Cosimo's lips trailing up her spine. She smiled and opened her eyes as he reached her lips. "Good morning, gorgeous. Oh, no fair, you brushed your teeth."

Cosimo chuckled. "You taste heavenly."

Biba rolled onto her back, and Cosimo immediately blew a raspberry on her stomach, making her giggle. "Silly boy." She combed her fingers through his messy dark curls, not really believing she was here in his bed, wrapped in his arms. "Cos?"

"Yeah, baby." He was kissing her breasts now, teasing her nipples into hard peaks.

"Is this really happening?"

Cosimo looked up, smiling. "It really is. It is happening. We are happening. I love you, Biba May."

"As I love you, Cosimo DeLuca." She hesitated. "Should we… keep this quiet?"

"Hmm." Cosimo propped himself up on his elbow next to her. "I've been wondering the same thing. There're pros and cons to both sides, but I think we could plow some middle path.

Don't announce it, but don't deny it. I want to hold your hand whether I'm in public or private."

"Stella's going to be mad."

"That's her problem. If she gets nasty, remember, the studio pays your salary. You won't be fired either way."

"Thank you. It's weird, but I don't feel guilty about this. I fell in love with you; Stella just wanted you for a conquest."

Cosimo made a face. "Yup, and if she'd done her homework, she'd know I don't roll that way. I've never been a playboy regardless of what people might think. I'm not saying I was a saint."

Biba grinned at him. "I should hope not. Have you seen you? What a waste if you were a monk."

Cosimo laughed. "You're very kind." He brushed her lips with his. "You want some breakfast?"

"I want some Cosimo..."

They made love again, enjoying every sensation that flowed through their bodies, then once more in the shower, slipping and sliding in the cubicle, laughing so much they eventually ended up on the cool tile floor.

Dressing, Biba gave a rueful grin. "I should have thought ahead and brought fresh underwear. I'll have to commando it back to my room."

"Damn, woman." Cosimo pointed to his cock which was getting hard at that thought, and Biba giggled.

"Then come over here, big boy."

SHE FINALLY MADE it back to her room to find a message from Stella on her phone. "Where the hell are you? It's Monday, Biba. Time to work."

Madam Snark. But Stella couldn't ruin Biba's happiness, and when Cosimo held her hand as they walked downstairs and out to the craft service trailer for breakfast, she didn't care who saw them or what they thought. There was a twinge of guilt when she saw Rich check out their linked hands, but he winked and smiled, and her unease lifted.

To their credit, no one made a big deal of Cosimo and Biba's obvious togetherness, and when they began work, they all switched back into their professional roles.

Biba went to find Stella. "Hey, Stel."

She waited for the bitchfest to begin, but Stella was subdued. "You okay, Stella?"

Stella nodded, then shook her head. "No, not really."

She looked so genuinely depressed that Biba sat down with her, taking her hand. "What is it?"

Stella handed her the iPhone she used for personal business only. "Look."

Biba opened the text message.

My love, soon we will be together, and the whole world will just melt away. You and I will be at peace—I promise you, it won't hurt for long, and then we'll be together for eternity. I love you. I want you. This is our fate, our destiny. Don't fight this, please. You have no idea what I'm capable of if anyone tries to get in our way. Yours, forever xxx

"Jesus." Biba felt sick, and Stella nodded.

"He's going to kill me. What else could he mean?"

Biba wanted to reassure her, but she knew it wasn't possible. The stalker's meaning was clear. She looked up and saw a tear escape Stella's eye. "I'm scared, Beebs."

Biba wrapped her arms around her boss and held her as she sobbed out all her fear. Stella was never this vulnerable in front of her, ever. She must be terrified, Biba thought. She leaned her cheek against Stella's blonde head. "We'll contact the FBI again, Stel. Cos won't let anything happen to you, I swear."

Stella sniffed and sat up. She gave Biba a strange smile. "Cos, is it now?"

Biba nodded. She held Stella's gaze, and finally Stella nodded. "Oh. I see."

"I'm sorry, Stella. It just happened."

Stella shrugged. "Don't apologize. You wanted him, you got him. All's fair and all that." She pulled at her bottom lip, in thought. "I'd been thinking anyway that I might just...take a break—from men, from relationships."

"You should. You have so much more to offer than just fucking randoms. You deserve more." Biba flushed at her outburst—would it sound like she was just relieved Stella wouldn't go after Cosimo?

But Stella just nodded. "You're right. Look, my eyes are disgustingly puffy now."

"Cold spoons and some cream, they'll be fine. You're not scheduled until this afternoon, anyway."

Stella was watching her. "I'm sorry about all the times I treated you badly, Biba. Like that message this morning. I was just in a bate."

Biba grinned. "I'm used to it."

Stella laughed a little. "I didn't use to be like this, you know. Before, I was sweet." She sighed. "But in this business, the things you see, the things you're forced to do...it's such a relief to be on this film set, you know? Working with a director of Cosimo's talent, his kindness, his...protection. You must feel that."

"I do."

"I'm sorry again about Damon."

"Not your fault, Stel. Look, let's have a chill out for a half hour, get you relaxed, and then we'll tackle this," she held up the iPhone, "together. We'll call the FBI and get to the bottom of this."

Special Agent Luke Harris arrived just after lunch, and he gathered Cosimo, Lars, Channing, Rich and Gunter, Stella and Biba, and Reg into the manor's large drawing room. Reggie nudged Biba. "Is Poirot going to tell us which one of us is a wrong 'un?"

Biba had to hide her snort of laughter as a cough.

Luke Harris took the photos on Stella's iPhone into evidence. "We'll process these as soon as possible. We'll need your fingerprints, Ms. May and Ms. Reckless for comparison."

"No problem."

Cosimo shifted irritably. "So, there's been no progress on the case?"

Luke Harris shook his head. "Whoever this is knows what he's doing. Ms. Reckless, we need to have a long conversation about your personal life, I'm afraid."

Stella grimaced. "It's all on Wikipedia. Can't you look it up?"

"I'm afraid not. And, I think you should know...Mr. Tracy's got good lawyers. He got the attempted rape charge dropped."

"What?" Cosimo was outraged, as Biba went pale. "What the hell? Why weren't we informed before?"

Harris shook his head. "I don't know, I'm sorry. Wherever Tracy fled to, he's well-hidden."

"This could be him." Cosimo shot a worried glance towards Biba. Harris nodded.

"Believe me, we have him on our suspect list. The only thing that prevents me from making him our number one suspect is that his motive would likely be revenge, not obsession, and I would think he would target Ms. May, rather than Ms. Reckless. To shut her up, so to speak."

"Jesus," Reggie hissed, his hand on Biba's shoulder, and even Harris looked apologetic.

"Sorry," he said to Biba, "that came out wrong. But I stand by my argument. I don't think this is him, which isn't to say you shouldn't be vigilant."

"This set is rapidly turning into a prison," Lars murmured to Cosimo. Cosimo's face was strained.

"Look, Agent Harris, we need to communicate better. Rich and Gunter are leading a strong team now, but you've seen this place. The woods around the lake, the openness of the manor itself…an army couldn't protect every inch. If someone gets in…I don't even want to think about what could happen."

Everyone in the room felt a chill creep down their spine, and when Biba looked in Cosimo's eyes, all she could see was fear.

## CHAPTER FOURTEEN

Agent Harris left after a little while without making any real assurances. Lars, Cosimo, and Channing went into a huddle, and the others drifted away. Biba had her arm around a quiet Stella as they made their way back to set. "You alright?"

Stella shook her head but didn't say anything. She leaned against Biba, and Biba knew she needed comfort more than anything else. "Come on, Stel. We'll go grab some hot chocolate and play some cards."

Stella shook her head. "I'm grateful, Biba, but I think I'd rather be alone for a while."

Biba watched her walk back to her trailer. Reggie massaged the back of his neck. "And here I thought this was going to be a relaxed, happy set."

Biba didn't smile. There was no doubt that this whole stalker thing cast a gloom over everyone. Both Rich and Gunter's demeanors, which were usually so fun-loving, were now quite cowed and defeated.

. . .

A FEW DAYS LATER, Reggie came to find her. "Pooks...I've got bad news."

"More?" Biba was tired and stressed out worrying for Stella.

"My mom's sick. I'm going to have to go up to see her on the weekend, instead of spending your birthday with you."

Biba hugged him. "That's no problem, boo, you have to be with Mary. What's up with her?"

"A virus, I think. She went up to the cabin in the mountains to paint and caught a cold that she can't shake."

"Oh, poor thing. Do you want me to come with you?"

Biba had known Mary for years. Ever since Reggie and she had become friends, Mary had been a pseudo-mother to her—kind, comforting, and fun-loving like her son. Mary had always hoped that Reggie and Biba would get together, but somehow, they'd gone from new acquaintances to best friends without ever going through the 'could we be more?' stage.

Reggie smiled at her. "No, it's okay. But she might appreciate a call if you have time."

Biba was already pulling her phone out of her pocket and dialing, "Mary Moo, you have the flu?"

She put it on speaker, so Reggie could listen, too. Mary Quinn chuckled, her voice hoarse and croaky. "Biba, how lovely to hear from you, darling. Yes, I'm afraid so. Damn thing won't shift. Reggie's insisting on coming to see me."

"And so he should. Shall I come, too?"

"Oh, no, dear. It's your birthday, and I don't want to risk infecting both of you. Besides, Reggie tells me you have a new man in your life."

Biba grinned, her body relaxing at the mention of Cosimo. "You would love him, Moo, truly."

"He's a handsome chap. I Googled him when Reggie told me who he was working for... yes, a very pretty boy. Those eyes. Lucky girl."

"I am that," Biba said. "Are you sure there's nothing I can get for you?"

"No, darling, Reggie's been more than kind. Maybe next year, we can all spend your birthday together."

"I would love that. Feel better soon, Moo. Love you."

"I love you, too, sweet girl."

Biba ended the call and smiled at Reggie. "If I haven't already said a million times, you are so lucky to have a mother like her."

"I think so, too." Reggie chewed his lip. "I do worry about her being in the mountains. Cinnamon Lodge is fine in the summer, but at this time of year, it gets below freezing up there, and if she's already sick..."

"She has heating, right? And the place is like a palace." Reggie and his mother weren't exactly poor. Reggie's father had made his fortune in textiles, and Reggie had never wanted for anything. Biba knew he worried about his mom being alone, but Mary Quinn was nothing if not independent.

"Well, if she won't let me visit, I'm at least going to send her a care package. You think you could bring it to her for me?"

Reggie smiled at her. "You're the sweetest, and of course."

Biba swung by that afternoon to go to a well-known Tacoma candy store. She spent a pleasurable hour choosing from the handmade chocolates, knowing Mary had a sweet tooth, then drove to the Tacoma Mall to find other little gifts for her de facto 'Mom'.

It wasn't until she left one store with a comfortable woolen blanket for Mary that Biba realized she was being followed. It started with a sick feeling inside as she felt someone walking too close behind her. She darted into the nearest store and circled back on herself to see if she could spot who it was.

No one. Was she being paranoid? Biba took a deep breath in and went out into the mall again. Ten minutes later, she got that same prickling up her spine and turned around. She was being paranoid. No one was paying any attention to her.

Shaking her head, she went to grab a coffee and saw Rich Furlough in the back of the shop, latte on the table in front of him, flicking through something on his phone. Biba hesitated for a moment. Would Rich have followed her?

He looked up then, and if he was acting, he did a good impression of being surprised. "Hey, short-stack, didn't expect to see you here. Can I get you a drink?"

Biba, not wanting to be rude, nodded. "I'd like that. Hot chocolate, please."

She settled down in the easy chair opposite Rich's and then laughed when he returned with a fully loaded hot chocolate for her. "I got them to put everything on—and I remembered you like a shot of vanilla syrup, too."

Biba relaxed. Rich was the last person she needed to be scared of. "Thank you, honey." She looked at the cream piled high on top of the liquid. "How on earth do I tackle this?"

"I suggest rappelling up the north face," Rich nodded sagely.

Biba giggled. "You are a lunatic." She took a sip, burying her nose in the cream, then giving him a wide grin. Rich laughed, shaking his head.

"Goddamn, May, stop being so adorable."

Biba felt slightly awkward. "Sorry."

"Dork. Adorkable."

Her shoulders eased. "That isn't a word."

"Is. So…?"

"So?"

"Elephant in the room. You and Cos—happy?"

She nodded firmly. "Very. I'm really sor—"

"Don't you dare say you're sorry, Beebs. I'm delighted for you, I really am. You and Cos make sense."

"Even with the age gap?"

"Fuck the age gap. Literally, ha ha." He grinned, and she couldn't help but laugh.

"What about you?"

Rich shrugged. "As everyone says, I have my life partner in Gunter, the goof ball." He grinned. "If only I was like Reggie."

"Huh?"

"Gay. Then me and Gun could have a happy life together."

Biba sipped her hot chocolate. "Reggie's not gay, Rich."

"Really?" Rich seemed genuinely taken aback, and Biba shook her head.

"Nope."

"Dang it. Now I owe Gun twenty bucks."

Biba laughed. "Oh, so you were fishing?"

Rich grinned. "Sorry. Just neither of us could figure out why you and Reggie never got together."

"There are some men who can resist me," she said, rolling her eyes. "Most men, actually."

"Ha. No chance."

She blew a raspberry, embarrassed at his compliment, and Rich laughed. He really was the sweetest guy. "What about Stella, Rich? She's single at the moment."

Rich raised both his hands. "Woah."

"Too much woman for you?"

"Too much drama for me. Nah, I'll just wait until they perfect cloning and borrow some of your DNA."

"Shucks. You know I snore like a walrus, right?"

"Stop."

"And I drool. Constantly. I look like the Swamp Creature in the mornings."

"Don't believe you."

Biba grinned wickedly "And I fart. A lot. Ask Stella. I'm always laying an air biscuit for her to find."

Rich was laughing so hard now his eyes were watering. "Stop! Oww, now I have a cramp."

Biba laughed at him as he calmed himself down. "God, it feels good to laugh after that crapola meeting the other day."

"Right? That FBI agent is a tool."

Biba nodded. "This whole thing is making me paranoid. Before I came in here, I could have sworn someone was following me. I even ducked into a couple of stores and double backed. Didn't see anyone, but I was spooked for a time."

Rich's smile had disappeared. "What the hell? Why didn't you lead with that?" He pushed back his chair, and Biba got up in alarm.

"What are you doing?"

He took her hand. "Come on. I'm friendly with the security team here. We're going to check out the mall security cameras.

## CHAPTER FIFTEEN

Cosimo was waiting for them when Rich drove her back to the set. Biba went into his arms, and he could feel her trembling. Rich was stone-faced. He nodded at Cosimo. "Someone followed Biba. A man, we think, but he or she was hooded."

Cosimo felt sick. Anything could have happened to Biba... "Did he have a weapon?"

He heard Biba, whose face was buried in his sweater, give a distressed squeak.

"It's okay, baby, you're safe," he said, burying his face in her hair, breathing her in.

"We couldn't tell. Thinking dispassionately about this, and that's not easy, but he would have nothing to gain by hurting Biba. I think it was just designed to either gather information or to spook us. Both, maybe."

Cosimo cursed. "Okay, from now, no one goes out alone. I don't want to run your lives, but while you work for me, all of you, you will be protected. Go in twos or take a security guard with you. That includes you and Gun, Rich. I don't think this guy is messing around."

"I agree." Rich put his hand on Biba's shoulder. "Beebs, I promise. You're safe."

Cosimo tilted Biba's chin up so she could see his face. He tried to smile. "What he said."

RICH LEFT THEM ALONE, and Cosimo took Biba back to his suite. He couldn't wait before taking her in his arms and kissing her. "God help me, if anyone ever hurts you…"

"It's not me he's after, Cos. Let's just focus on that. Although poor Stella. I cannot imagine how she must feel at the moment."

"I know. She was quiet again today. I think Franco and Sifrido were going to take her to dinner and try to make her feel better."

"Good guys."

Cosimo smiled. "They are." He cupped her face in his hand. "Thank God you're okay."

"I am, now." She leaned into his big body. He scooped her into his arms and sat down in the easy chair, with her cradled against him. Biba pressed her lips against his neck. "I'm scared for Stella."

"I know, honey." He kissed her. "But for tonight, she's okay. She's safe. And…" He suddenly smiled, "It's your birthday tomorrow."

"Twenty-two."

"Old lady."

Biba laughed. "Take this old lady to bed, boy."

They made love slowly, Biba straddling him as he caressed her breasts and belly. She rode him, impaling herself on his huge cock, sighing with ecstasy every time she sunk him inside her. "God, I'll never get tired of this, Cosimo. Never."

"Me neither, baby. God, yes, that's it, when you clench your cunt around me like that…"

Biba's eyes were dancing, clearly reveling in the power she had over him at moments like this. "You mean, like this?"

She clenched her vaginal muscles and her thighs, and he groaned with pleasure. Biba grinned, running her hands up and down his chest and stomach. "You are such a gorgeous man," she murmured and leaned down to kiss him, nipping at his bottom lip with her teeth.

Cosimo grabbed her buttocks in his hands, fingers digging into her soft flesh. Biba looked down at him. "You want to...?"

He was surprised. "You want to try anal sex?"

"With you, I want to try anything."

"For instance?"

Biba smiled. "You could...restrain me. Tie me up. Have your wicked way."

Cosimo grinned. "You surprise me every day, Biba May. Hey, that rhymed."

"Goofball, and yes... I like the idea of being at your mercy. Maybe some light spanking?"

Cosimo, so turned on by her talk, suddenly flipped her onto her back and began to thrust hard. "You drive me crazy, Miss May..."

She clung to him as they made love long into the night, then, wrapped in each other's arms, they slept until mid-morning.

The next morning, Biba opened her eyes and started to laugh immediately. Next to her, Cosimo lay, naked and glorious, wearing a glitter-covered paper hat with a party horn in his mouth. He blew into it, and the curled paper tongue rolled out and bopped her on the nose. Biba giggled.

"You lunatic."

Cosimo took the party favor from his mouth and leaned in to kiss her. "Happy birthday, Snooks."

"Snooks?"

"New nickname."

Biba considered. "I'll allow it."

Cosimo grinned. "So, Miss May, I have plans for you today—but only if they sound good to you."

"Hit me."

"Breakfast in bed, all your favorites. Then a long, sexy soak in the tub—with me of course. The crew and cast have organized a special lunch for you."

"That's sweet—and I love how much of this day revolves around food."

"And sex. Don't forget the sex."

"How could I?" She giggled as he wrapped his arms around her and kissed her neck. "After lunch?"

"After lunch, we get some alone time. We're going to Gig Harbor…and we're going on a gondolier—if I can't take you to Venice—yet—then I'm bringing Venice to you."

Biba looked excited. "That's so romantic, babe. God, how lovely."

Cosimo grinned, obviously pleased. "Afterwards, a romantic dinner for two in the city, then back here for a little surprise out on the lake."

"You really have organized this," Biba said, touched beyond belief. This man truly loved her.

Cosimo covered her body with his, grinning down at her. "I'll admit, Reggie helped me out some. I'm sorry he won't be here to help us celebrate."

"Me, too… I'm sure he wishes he was, too, but his mom means a lot to both of us."

"Snooks?"

"Yeah?"

"Let's not talk about Reggie's mom when I'm trying to mount you."

Biba laughed aloud, then sighed happily as Cosimo sank his cock deep inside her. They made love slowly, tenderly until both were panting for air and shuddering through intense orgasms.

Cosimo meant it when he said breakfast with all of her favorites. Granola, scrambled eggs, pancakes, French toast, and fresh fruit. Biba had a good-sized portion of every item, much to Cosimo's amusement.

"Listen, man, I need the energy," Biba said, chomping half a pancake in one go. "You constantly demanding sex from me..."

She giggled as Cosimo tried to tickle her. "Don't eat too much...I don't need you throwing up on me when we make love."

"Ha ha..." But she put down the rest of her pancake and climbed onto his lap. "Thank you. Thank you for a wonderful birthday."

"It's not even begun yet," he said with a smile, and kissed her with such passion that they forgot all about the food and tumbled to the carpet, laughing and kissing until they were breathless.

STELLA DELETED the email and sat back, pissed. She'd lost out on another role to Jennifer Lawrence, and now she was fuming. Yes, she was JLaw's senior by ten years, but the character they had been up for was in her late thirties, like Stella.

What was worse was that they shared an agent which meant Dan Flint was pushing Jennifer more than he was Stella—probably because they'd pay more for Jen, and his cut would be bigger. Stella was old enough and smart enough to know that made sense, but where was his sense of loyalty? Stella had made him a millionaire several times over, and, more importantly, a power player in Hollywood.

Stella tapped out another cigarette. It killed her appetite, but lately, she had begun to wonder if the constant starvation and working out was worth it for the roles she was getting. Except this one, of course. She had planned on this movie being the one which kick-started her career again. She might be the biggest movie star on the planet, but when you were at the top, there was only one way to go...down.

She scrubbed at her face with her hands. Christ, she was only thirty-six, but she felt a decade older. Maybe it was from being with someone as young as Biba all the time. Stella wasn't someone who had female friends, and her own mother was estranged from her. The older Reckless had written a tell-all about her daughter five years previously which nearly torpedoed Stella's career with its revelations of teen pregnancy and abortions. Biba was the closest person to Stella, not that Stella would admit that. Which is why, honestly, when Stella needed to lash out, Biba bore the brunt.

Stella's biggest fear in life was being too close to someone—and then losing them. It stemmed from her losing her beloved Pa when she was eight, suddenly in a fiery car wreck. She had been pulled from the car at the last moment and had heard his screams as he died. They stayed with her. So, when she found herself softening towards her long-term assistant, she drew back and got extra bitchy with Biba.

Now, as she stepped from her trailer and walked back to the manor, she saw Biba and Cosimo hand-in-hand, so obviously joyful in their love for each other. Stella again felt the jolt just as she had when she first realized Cosimo and Biba were falling for each other. It hurt. She hated to admit it, but it hurt like hell that she had been passed over for Biba.

And then there was Biba's wild, untamed beauty. Stella wished she had the natural freshness Biba had, the utter lack of reliance on makeup, instead harnessing all the vitality of youthful spirit. Stella wished she didn't care as much over her own appearance; she knew she was beautiful but in an ice queen way, not the soft, sensual, breath of fresh air way that Biba inhabited.

She ignored Biba and Cosimo as they made their way to see the other members of cast and crew. Franco kissed Biba's cheek, and Sifrido twirled her in his arms. Jesus. Stella's lip curled up in a sneer.

When Biba came over to her, Stella turned cold eyes on her. "Aren't we the center of attention?"

She pushed the guilt aside when she saw Biba's face fall a little. Biba quickly picked herself up though. "And good morning to you, too. I was going to see if you wanted to join Cos and I and some of the others for lunch."

"No, thanks."

Biba stared at her, and her eyes turned cold. "Fine." She stalked off, and Stella sighed. What was the point of that? It was Biba's birthday, for Chrissakes, why shouldn't she be feted and celebrated? *God, I'm turning into such an old movie star bitch cliché.* She turned to call out after Biba, to wish her a happy birthday, but Biba was already halfway across the site, her arm around Cosimo's waist.

*Shit. I'm sorry, Biba. But I can't show how much you mean to me. If I do, I'll lose all the power in our relationship.*

Stella grabbed some black coffee and went to work.

## CHAPTER SIXTEEN

They filmed until lunchtime. Rich and Gunter had set up a barbecue in the grounds—greasy, smoky, saucy—Biba loved it. She felt a little overwhelmed by all the attention and wasn't quite sure how to process the affection these people had for her.

She took a moment alone to decompress and called Reggie.

"Hey, birthday girl."

Biba relaxed. "Hey, Boo. How's your mom?"

"She's okay, a bit sniffy and moaning like a be-otch about it."

"I heard that," came a voice in the background, and both Biba and Reggie laughed.

"Mom says happy birthday, too, and thank for the care package. Jesus, so much sugar, Beebs, are you trying to make my mom diabetic? There's fifteen packs of Red Vines."

Biba grinned. "She likes them."

"Good grief. Are you being spoiled today?"

"So much...Cos told me you organized most of it, so thank you."

"Nah, it was teamwork. Enjoy it, boo."

Biba chuckled, but Reggie must have picked up on something in her tone. "What is it, Beebs?"

Biba swallowed a lump in her throat. "I've just...it's like having a family again."

Reggie's voice softened. "We love you, silly girl. Of course we're your family. Listen, I've got a gift for you, but I don't think I'll be home tomorrow. Probably Tuesday or something."

"Dude, don't worry about it. I miss you, but your mom is more important. Tell her I love her, won't you?"

"I will. Happy birthday, darling."

Cosimo had another surprise in store for her...they were going to Gig Harbor by helicopter. As they flew over Ruston and Shore Acres, Biba kissed Cosimo. "You are the best gift any woman could have."

Cosimo grinned. "Ha, tell me again on our fiftieth wedding anniversary when I'm ninety, and you're still spritely and active. You'll trade me in for a younger model."

"Well, of course," Biba tried to keep a straight face. "But I think you overestimate how long I'll wait to take a younger lover."

Cosimo grinned. "Oh, really? Damn, I was banking on at least fifty years."

They both laughed, and Cosimo locked his fingers with hers. "God, you make me happy, Biba May."

"Right back at you, handsome."

Cosimo beamed then nodded out of the helicopter's window. "We're here."

THEY BOTH AGREED that the gondolier ride was incredibly romantic, but over dinner in one of the most exclusive restaurants in the city, Cosimo expressed his true love for his hometown of Venice. "It is the most incredible place to grow up. We used to take Nicco every summer. Grace and I always followed the rule of when one works, the other doesn't. But in the summer, we always managed a month together in Venice. When Nicco grew up, of course, he wanted to spend summers with his friends, so the trips back home trailed off."

"Did your own mother never live there?"

"Only when I was young."

Biba studied him. "You never mention your dad."

Cosimo sipped his wine and shrugged. "Because I never knew him. Mom got pregnant by a married man—she didn't know he was married—and decided to raise me on her own. We even lived in a women-led commune for a time in France before we came here."

"And she's American?"

Cosimo nodded. "Washingtonian born and bred."

"I can't wait to meet her."

Cosimo kissed her hand. "She will adore you, Biba."


WHEN THEY GOT BACK to Lakewood, Biba saw that the little beach next to the lake was lit up with tiki torches, and a thrill ran through her. "What have you mad people done now?"

Cosimo laughed. "Wait and see."

Their friends and colleagues greeted them, and she saw Rich nod to Cosimo with a grin.

"Now?"

"Now," agreed Cosimo, and he took Biba's hand, smiling down at her. "Happy birthday, baby."

Biba nearly jumped out of her skin as fireworks began streaking through the night sky and exploding in a riot of colors above them. She laughed and shook her head. "You did all this for me?"

Cosimo kissed her tenderly. "You are so loved, Biba, not just by me. By Reggie, by Rich, by the rest of them...even Stella loves you."

"Ha."

"She does. She just likes to hide it." He looked around for the blonde actress, but Stella was nowhere to be seen. "Hey, Rich, someone being a diva still?"

Rich slung his arm around Biba's shoulders. "Stel's been sulking all afternoon, hiding out in her trailer. Want me to go find her?"

Biba shook her head, but Cosimo rolled his eyes. "Yes, go find her. Tell her to stop being a mean girl and come out to play."

Rich chuckled. "Will do."

Biba sighed. "Cos, this day has been magical, just magical. Thank you, baby."

Cosimo's cell phone rang, and he grinned as he saw who was calling. "I think this is for you, Beebs." He handed her his phone, and Biba said "Hello?"

"Happy Birthday!" Nicco sang it down the phone, and Biba laughed.

"Hey, Nic, thank you so much for calling. Your dad has been spoiling me all day."

"He said he was going to—how was the gondolier?"

Biba laughed. "Amazing. But you've done the real thing, huh?"

"Not for a while. Maybe we could all go to Venice in the summer...oh, hey, Grandma wants to say hi."

Biba's heart beat a little faster as a gentle voice said hello. "Hello, Mrs. DeLuca. It's wonderful to meet—or speak—to you."

Olivia DeLuca laughed. "It's Olivia, and I've heard so many good things about you. Happy birthday, dear."

"Thank you so much." Biba's nerves soon dissolved as she

chatted with Cosimo's mother for a few minutes, then Nicco came back on the phone.

"Yeah, like I was saying, maybe we could all go to Venice in the summer. It's a cool place—lots of stuff I can show you."

"Sounds good to me, Nic. Do you want to speak to your dad?"

"Yeah, please. Happy birthday again, Beebs, see you soon."

As she handed Cosimo's phone back to him, Biba felt like her entire being was buzzing with joy. She felt like she had a family now—Cosimo's son and mother accepting her so readily. She felt tears pop into her eyes, and as Cosimo ended his call, he swept his finger along her cheekbone, capturing the water.

"Happy tears," she said, "I promise. I can't believe this is all happening, Cos. I love you so much."

Cosimo took her into his arms. "You have changed my world, Biba, from a place of darkness to one of light. I love you."

Biba couldn't see how she could ever be unhappy again, but within the hour they would all be shown that sometimes worlds can shatter in the blink of an eye.

## CHAPTER SEVENTEEN

As they walked hand-in-hand back toward the manor, Biba looked over to the trailers. She could see a faint light coming from the largest, and she knew Stella was sulking in her trailer. She nudged Cosimo. "I'm going to go make peace with Stella," she said. "I feel bad about our argument."

Cosimo sighed. "Baby, Stella needs to grow up some and realize not everything is about her."

"I know, but I feel bad."

Cosimo stopped. "Want me to come?"

Biba kissed him. "I think you being there might make matters worse. I knew she wasn't okay with us. I think that's what her tantrum was about, really."

"She'll have to get used to it." Cosimo leaned his forehead against hers. "I love you."

Biba smiled. "I love you, too, Cosimo DeLuca. Thank you for a perfect birthday."

"Don't be too long."

"I promise."

. . .

THE RAIN HAD BEGUN to pour down now, and Biba walked quickly toward the trailers and made her way through the maze of them to Stella's. As she turned towards it, she almost fell over a prone figure on the ground. "Hey!"

In the dim light, she saw it was Rich. "Man, how much did you have to drink, Richyboy?"

He was lying face down and didn't even groan when she poked him with her toe. "Rich?"

She managed to hoist him over onto his back—and gasped. The front of his T-shirt was covered in blood. Biba recoiled. "Oh my God... help! Somebody help us! Rich? Rich, c'mon man, wake up."

Then she heard Stella scream, and in horror, saw a dark figure wrestling a naked and screaming Stella out of her trailer.

"No!" Biba launched herself at them, her body knocking the figure away from her boss. The rain made it slippery, and the attacker stumbled as Biba pounded on his back. Stella was frozen in horror.

"Stella! Run!" Biba screamed it at her as the attacker threw her off and reached for Stella. Biba wasn't about to let her boss be snatched, and she body-slammed the attacker. She heard shouts coming from the direction of the manor. "Stella, run! Cosimo's coming..."

The assailant grabbed her by the throat with one hand and slammed her back against the trailer. He drove his fist into her stomach twice—vicious blows—and Biba crumpled, the wind knocked out of her.

She dragged in some air into her lungs, watching the attacker clutch a crawling Stella and drag her away. When Biba tried to rise and follow them, her legs would not work. She could hear Cosimo shouting her name.

"I'm here..." but her voice wouldn't work either, and now a wave of dizziness hit her. The pain from the blows wasn't dissipating at all—in fact it was getting worse. Biba managed to stagger up and lurch a couple of steps just as lights came on, and Cosimo burst onto the scene. Biba saw the horror in his eyes, and she pointed to Rich. "Help him."

But Cosimo was running towards her, screaming her name, and Biba looked down. Now she knew why his face looked so full of horror. The hilt of a knife protruded from her belly, her white dress turning red and pink. She looked up into Cosimo's distraught green eyes as her legs finally failed her, and he caught her as she fell.

"He stabbed me?" she said, incredulously, and shook her head. "He's taken Stella, Cos. He's taken Stella."

The pain was growing worse, and black spots danced in her vision. I'm dying. We had no time, no time.

"I love you," she said, touching Cosimo's face, and then all was silent.

## CHAPTER EIGHTEEN

Two years previously, Cosimo DeLuca sat by his dying wife's bedside and held her hand as she gently slipped away, another victim of cancer. He had thought it was the worst day of his life.

It was nothing to the terror he felt now. Waiting and covered in the blood of his twenty-two-year-old lover, having been told to stay behind in the waiting room. Both Biba and Rich had been rushed to the emergency room; the FBI and police were all over Lakewood and the hospital; and journalists were clamoring outside for the news.

Rich was in bad, bad shape—multiple stab wounds to the chest. Gunter was inconsolable. But all Cosimo could think about was Biba: her wan face, the blood pumping from her wounds. He'd lain her on the wet ground and pressed down hard on the savage wounds in her belly, trying to keep her blood inside her. They had to pry him away from her when the first responders arrived.

His Biba. His beautiful, spirited, fun-loving Biba was dying, and there was nothing he could do about it.

The police had taken her and Rich's details and told them

they would contact next-of-kin. Cosimo wondered if Biba's parents would care. He told the police to go find Reggie—he was the closest to a family she had—except for, now, Cosimo himself.

Cosimo had called his mother, telling her what happened. "Mom, I have to tell Nicco—he cannot hear this on the news."

"Dad?"

Cosimo nearly broke down when he heard his son. "Nicco... Biba's hurt. There was an incident—Stella was abducted, and Rich and Biba were hurt trying to stop him."

There was a hushed silence, then Nicco spoke, and his voice was gravelly with shock. "Is she okay?"

"No, son, she's not. She was stabbed. They're operating on her now.

"I'll come down."

Cosimo almost panicked. "No. No, Nic, really. You don't want to be here, it's...hell."

"Dad." The way Nicco's voice trembled broke Cosimo's heart.

"I promise, I swear, if she gets worse...I'll call you straight away. I promise on my life, Nicco."

Another long pause. "Okay. Tell her to fight, Pa. She can do it if anyone can. I know it."

"Thank you, buddy. She will fight...that's Biba's way."

"Love you, Daddy."

Cosimo did break down then. "Love you too, Nic. Please, pray for her."

He took himself away to sob in private, then returned to the waiting room to sag down onto the couch. Lars put his arm around Cosimo's shoulders. "Keep hope, Cos. Keep hope."

An hour later, they came to tell them that Rich was dead.

BIBA WOKE up hyperventilating and tried to sit up, only to be pushed back down by firm hands. "Sweetheart, you can't sit up. Take sips of air...that's it...focus on my face." A man's face, covered in a surgical mask, loomed into her vision. "It's okay, Biba, you're safe. You're okay. You're in the recovery room at Sacred Heart Medical Center."

Another gentle hand was stroking her forehead. Another face—a nurse, smiled down at her. "You've done well, Biba. We're just keeping an eye on you...you lost a lot of blood."

"Stabbed." She croaked from underneath an oxygen mask, and the woman nodded.

"I know, baby girl, I'm sorry."

"Stella?"

Biba saw them look at each other. "We don't know about anything apart from you, Biba. We know your partner is waiting on some news. I'm just going to tell him about your surgery."

"Want to see him."

"As soon as you're stable, hon."

Biba nodded, feeling so out of it she could barely concentrate. She wondered why she felt no pain, then remembered they would have given her morphine. But she was alive.

Was Stella okay? What about Rich? How had the day gone from such joy to such horror?

Biba closed her eyes, feeling helpless. What the fuck was wrong with people?

She slept, fitfully at first, but then she sunk into a deep restful slumber, waking to bright sunshine which hurt her eyes, and a familiar hand held hers.

"Snooks?"

His voice made her relax; his nickname made her smile. "Cos..."

"Thank God, you're okay, baby. It's going to be okay." His green eyes were full of pain.

She reached out and stroked his cheek. "I'm okay. Stella?"

Cosimo seemed to struggle for a moment. "He took her. The FBI and the police have instigated a manhunt."

"God." Biba tried again to sit up again, and Cosimo helped her into position. Biba touched the heavy dressing on her abdomen. "How bad is it?"

"It could have been a lot worse. No major organs, but your artery was damaged. They've grafted it and seem confident you will recover quickly, but you'll need some more blood transfusions."

Cosimo told her all of this as if reciting what the doctors had told him gave him hope. Biba nodded.

"I honestly don't feel bad. A little pain."

Cosimo put the clicker in her hand. "Press this for the morphine." He let out a shaky breath. "Christ, Biba, when I saw you covered in blood, that knife sticking out of you...I thought I'd lost you."

"I'm still here." Biba reached out to tilt his chin up, make him look her in the eye. "Rich?"

She saw the grief in his eyes and moaned "Oh, no..." as Cosimo told her that Rich didn't make it. "Not Rich...God, Cos..." She began to weep, and he cradled her in his arms.

As her sobs slowed to a whimper, a doctor came in to see them. Biba could see the woman studying her for signs of pain or distress. She wiped her eyes. "I'm okay, Doc, just...a friend died."

"Mr. Furlough? I know. I'm so sorry for your loss. How are you feeling this morning, relatively speaking?"

Biba nodded. "Actually okay...more tired than anything."

The doctor made her lie back while she undid Biba's dressings and examined her wounds. Biba saw the jagged incisions and stitches on her belly; Cosimo turned away, looking sickened and angry at the same time. The doctor inspected the wounds. "We managed to repair the damage easily—no organ damage, which was the main concern. No signs of infection, which is good. The tiredness you're experiencing is because of the blood loss and trauma. You were a little anemic to start with—did you know that?"

Biba shook her head. "I didn't."

"Well, we're going to keep you in for a couple of days, and then you can go home to recover."

Biba was surprised. "So quickly?"

"You were very lucky. I'll check back with you later."

Both Biba and Cosimo thanked her, then Cosimo returned to sit by her. "You'll be staying in my hotel suite while you recover. Obviously, production has been shut down on the movie; we can't make it without Stella."

"God, I hope she's okay."

Cosimo shook his head. "I just pray we find her before that psycho does something stupid."


Stella wasn't nearly close to being okay. Her abductor had raged at her for 'making me hurt those people, making me kill that girl' as he had driven her away into the night, and she had cringed away from his terrifying wrath. At least he had tossed her a blanket to cover herself, and she wrapped it tightly around her body. It saved her modesty but didn't protect much from the biting cold.

"Where are you taking me?"

He didn't answer. He wore a black balaclava, and bizarrely, she had noticed his bright blue eyes—too blue. Contacts? His voice was disguised, too. He was hiding.

Stella felt sick. When she watched him stab Biba so mercilessly, watched her assistant—her friend—collapse, bloodsoaked, Stella had frozen, not believing what she was seeing. Oh Biba, I'm sorry, I'm so sorry. Stella wondered if she was dead.

She barely remembered him dragging her to his van. Now, with her hands bound behind her back, she lay on the freezing metal floor of a van as he drove it. She had the sense that they were going uphill, and with the cold, she guessed they were driving up a mountain. Maybe Rainier, or Olympic National Park. She had lost track of time; they could have been on the road for hours. Maybe he was even taking her to Canada.

"Please," she spoke softly. "Please tell me what you want."

Nothing. Silence. She changed track. "I'm very cold...sir. Could you possibly crank up the heat?"

Again, no reply, but she saw him turn the heat up. "Thank you." Good, that gave her hope that he had some humanity in him. She kept quiet then, trying to figure out how to deal with this. Should she give him what he wanted? Her love? Her body? Stella was a grown-up. If it took offering him these things to preserve her life, she would do it. Or should she try to exert power by turning on the diva in her? Would that mean he would kill her quicker?

What do you want? Tell me...

An hour later, the van came to an abrupt halt, and the man got out, coming around to the back of the vehicle. He yanked open the doors and grabbed her, wrapping a thick coat around her and picking her up easily. She had been right—they were in the mountains. Snow swirled around them, making it hard to see, but soon she realized he was taking her to a lodge of some kind. It was warmly lit, and Stella felt a little surge of hope.

But once inside, when she saw just what kind of monster he really was, all her hope died, and Stella Reckless began to scream.

## CHAPTER NINETEEN

Reggie, breathless and shaking, burst into Biba's hospital room, making both her and Cosimo jump. Reggie stared at her. "Oh, thank God...thank God..."

He threw himself at her, and Biba hugged him hard, wincing slightly at the force of his embrace. For a few minutes, she reassured him that she was fine; she was okay. Cosimo left them alone, shooting a smile at his lover before he left the room.

Reggie finally sat down on the chair Cosimo had vacated. "God, Biba...I'm sorry I'm so late. Mom got sicker and when Cosimo called...the I-5 had traffic backed up."

"It's okay, I'm fine," Biba said. She indicated a blood bag hanging above her. "Just getting some fresh stuff pumped into me." She gave Reggie a half smile, then it faded. "Rich is dead, Reg."

He nodded. "I know. God, I'm sorry...have they any news about Stella?"

"Nothing. Whoever took her had it planned out perfectly. At least that what's the FBI thinks."

Reggie sighed, shaking his head. "Agent Harris again?"

"Yup."

"Jesus...couldn't they have sent someone who wasn't a moron? Stella's life is in danger."

Biba's eyes filled with tears, and Reggie squeezed her hand. "I'm sorry, boo, I didn't mean to upset you. I just mean...God, I don't know."

"Cosimo's sending out private detectives to look for them. They have questions."

Reggie looked impressed. "Such as?"

"How the hell did the abductor get in past the gates? How did he know that Stella was alone in her trailer when the rest of us were out at the lake?" Biba sighed, rubbing her face with her fingers, hard enough to leave red marks. "Reg...who would do this? Murder Rich? Take Stella?"

"A psychopath, Beebs. That's the only thing I got." He nodded at her body. "Does it hurt?"

"It's sore, but bearable." Biba looked out of the window. "Gunter is absolutely destroyed, Reg. He came to see me yesterday...he's broken." Her voice shook.

Reggie shook his head, his eyes filled with sympathy. "I'm so sorry...Rich was one of the good ones."

"He was."

They sat in companionable silence for a while. "How's your mom doing?"

"Docs think it might be pneumonia now. She's pretty sick."

Biba groaned. "God. Reg, you need to go back to her. I'm okay here, seriously. If all goes well, I'll be out of here in a couple of days, and I have Cosimo to take care of me. Mary needs you."

He looked at her unhappily. "Are you sure?"

"Absolutely. Get back to her, Reggie. You can call me whenever you like."

He got up and hugged her again. "I love you."

"I love you, too," she told him, smiling. "Hey, and listen. Tell your Mom Red Vines are great for pneumonia."

Reggie rolled his eyes and chuckled. "I will...she won't need much persuasion. Later, Beebs. Glad you're feeling okay."

"Later, Reggie."

DOWNSTAIRS, Cosimo was talking to some of the nurses at the station. "It is customary that we ask the relative to donate blood," one of them was telling him.

"Of course. I have some right now if you could point me in the right direction."

"I'll come with you."

Cosimo turned around to see his mother, Olivia, and Nicco walking toward him. "Hey... Hey, you guys...why are you here?"

"You really think we're not going to come support you and Biba? I don't know my blood type though."

Cosimo hugged his son and mother. "Both your mom and I were O negative, so you'll be, too."

"Ah, good," the nurse said, "the universal blood donor. We will check it though. We always do before a first-time donation. Come with me."

As they walked, Nicco bombarded Cosimo with questions. "Is Biba okay? Have they found Stella?"

"Yes and no," Cosimo said as they made their way to the blood donation room. "The FBI are out hunting, but there's no news. Biba is doing well—actually, better than hoped. She'll be delighted to see you both."

THEY FILLED out the preliminary paperwork, and all three of them had their blood types taken. As they waited to give blood, Cosimo tried to relax. It had been such a fraught day and a half that he felt as if he hardly drawn breath.

The nurse came in, looking perplexed. "We're going to have

to do your blood type again, young man," she said, "we think we've got a bad reading."

Nicco shrugged. "Sure, no problem."

Twenty minutes later, the doctor came to see them. His face serious. "Can I just double check some details?"

"Sure."

He asked Cosimo about Nicco's birth and the circumstances surrounding it. Both Cosimo and Nicco exchanged confused looks. Olivia took charge.

"Doctor, give it to us straight. What are you saying?"

The doctor looked uncomfortable. "Mr. DeLuca, your son's blood type was tested five times by our nurses, and each time returned the same result. Blood type AB positive. There's no doubt."

Cosimo felt the blood drain from his face. "What?"

Nicco got it before his father and turned to them with a grim face. "They're saying I'm not your son, Dad. They're saying Mom cheated on you..."

## 20

# CHAPTER TWENTY

A week. That was all it was, but their lives had all changed immeasurably. Biba was discharged from the hospital after five days, and she and Cosimo went to his hotel in the city. The set at Lakewood had been deemed a crime scene, and the movie abandoned for now, so the cast and crew had decamped to the hotels. Each of them had been questioned about the night of Rich's murder and Stella's abduction. The national news media hounded their every step.

Cosimo managed to sneak Biba into the hotel through the service elevator. The news had learned that Cosimo and Biba were in a relationship and were fascinated by the story of dashingly handsome cinematic wunderkind and the all-American beauty he'd fallen in love with.

Cosimo was still reeling from the revelation of Nicco's parentage. Everything he had believed about his marriage crumbled around him. Worse, he was heartbroken, until Nicco, Olivia, and Biba had all told him the same thing. Nicco, in his teenage way, had put it best and bluntly. "I don't give a fuck whose DNA I've got...you're my father and fuck everyone else."

Biba had agreed with him. "Screw blood types. You raised him, Cos...Nicco is your son."

Now, alone with Biba in their hotel suite, Cosimo finally felt able to face what had happened. They lay together on the bed. Biba kissed him. "Seems weird to be in bed with you and not able to have sex. Are you sure the doctor said six weeks and not six hours?"

Cosimo chuckled. "Unfortunately so. But you need to heal. God, we were lucky it wasn't worse."

"I can't stop thinking about Stella and Rich. Rich deserved better. What do you think happened?"

"I think, like you, he arrived at the wrong time, just as the psycho was about to abduct Stella. Or maybe Rich got there just beforehand, and he was stabbed just to get him out of the way."

Biba looked sick. "I can't stop seeing the blood."

Cosimo stroked her face. "Try not to think about it." He pressed his lips to hers, feeling her respond. "Biba...when this is all over, I'd like to take you away to Italy—to just get some alone time. I feel in my bones that we'll get Stella back alive."

"How can you be so sure?"

He gave a humorless laugh. "I don't know."

There was a knock at the door, and Cosimo got up. It was their private security guard. "I'm sorry to disturb you, sir, but there are two military personnel here to see you."

Cosimo was confused as Biba sat up. "I don't know..."

"Let them in," Biba said in a strange voice, standing and coming to his side. "Please. Let them in."

Cosimo looked in confusion at her, but Biba's expression was hard as stone.

As the two visitors stepped into the suite—a man and a woman—Cosimo suddenly understood. Biba stiffened beside him. "Well," she said with a voice like ice, "Hi, Mom. Hi, Dad. To what do we owe the pleasure?"

Cosimo walked into the bar, and Sifrido and Franco waved him over. "How's Biba?"

"At the moment, hard to say. Her parents showed up...at last."

Sifrido whistled, but Franco nodded. "Good. It's about time."

Cosimo felt a hundred years old. "Tell me some good news." Sifrido had taken the lead in keeping in touch with the police investigation, while Lars and Channing dealt with the studio and the FBI.

"Well, if no news is good news..." Sifrido said, and Cosimo's shoulders slumped.

"Fuck. I just feel so useless. Can't we make a public appeal—something?"

"We could—but who knows if it would do any good?"

Cosimo sighed. "It's worth a shot. I'll talk to Lars and Chan. Maybe we can persuade Agent Doofus to help us."

"Maybe."

"I have to do something...how's Gunter doing?"

Franco sighed. "He quit, that's all we know for sure. He's going back to Germany as soon as he's allowed. Poor kid. Rich was his other half in so many ways. Sometimes we don't recognize that a deep friendship is just as profound as a romantic or familial one."

Upstairs in their suite, Biba was wondering who these people were to her now—these people standing in front of her. Lookswise, there was a smattering of grey hair, but otherwise they looked no different than the last time she had seen them.

"So, you've come." This was after all three of them had been silent for too long.

Her father cleared his throat. "You were hurt."

"Stabbed. Yes. I was in the hospital for five days. It was on the news, which is how I assume you found out about it." Biba wasn't in the mood to play nice.

"You could have called us." Her mother spoke finally, and Biba detected a little quaver to her voice. Her mother, the Major, was nervous of her. Biba didn't care.

"I could have, but then again I was busy recovering from being stabbed. Stabbed. Did you not understand that part?" She gave a disgusted noise. "Why are you here?"

Her father glanced at her mother, then cleared his throat. "We wanted to say...about Derek... We're sorry. We're sorry we didn't listen to you."

Biba stared at her father. "Derek was sent to jail five years ago. You've had five years to apologize, and yet it's been crickets. Why now?"

"Because..."

"Because I was stabbed? So now that I've almost been murdered, now I'm worthy of being apologized to? Shove your apology."

She turned away from them, not wanting them to see her tears, but her mother caught her arm.

"Biba...please. Listen to us."

Biba sighed. "You know what? Fine. I accept your apology. You're forgiven. But you'll have to excuse me. My friend was just murdered, and my boss—and friend—is missing, abducted by a psychopath who stuck his knife in my belly. Twice. I don't have time for reunions when my real family is suffering. Please, just go."

She turned away again and went back into the bedroom, shutting the door behind her but staying close to it to hear what they had decided to do. She heard low voices and the suite door being opened and shut. She peeked out and saw with relief that they had gone. She went to find the security guard and asked him where Cosimo had gone.

"I believe he is in the bar, Miss May. I'll escort you down."

STELLA TRIED to block the stench of death out of her nose with the blanket he had given her. At last he had allowed her to find something to wear. The woman who had lived here—the woman who stared back at Stella with sightless, dead eyes as she huddled in the tiny, locked bedroom—had been roughly Stella's size.

When he'd dragged Stella to the bedroom—her prison, it seemed—he'd pointed out the closet without saying anything. Stella was pathetically grateful for the clothes found—sweaters, jeans, fleeces, and socks. She'd pulled on everything she could find, layering clothes over clothes. The room itself was heated, the bed comfortable, and Stella had to admit, if she wasn't terrified for her life, she could pretend she was on a break.

But she was terrified, barely sleeping in case he forced himself on her. But he'd left her alone for long periods. Until now. This morning, he unlocked her door and made her come out into the living room. She tried not to look at the dead woman slumped in the easy chair, her blood-soaked shirt, the gaping slice in her neck, almost to the bone. The brutality of it made her shiver, reminded her—as if she needed reminding—of the way he had attacked Biba—the utter lack of mercy.

"Who was she?" Stella asked without thinking, but he ignored her. Stella swallowed and stepped towards the woman. "Can I close her eyes at least? Cover her up?"

"Leave her alone." The scarf tied over his face muffled his

voice, but he wasn't using the voice manipulator. Stella decided to try to get him to talk. If he was someone she knew…

Because she figured out—he had to be. To get through the security Cosimo had put in place at Lakewood, to be able to know exactly where her trailer was and to get in…

"Can we talk?" Stella decided to turn on the Reckless charm—what harm could it do? She averted her eyes from the evidence of the harm it could do—the dead woman—and sat down in another chair. "What is it we are doing here? Your letters said…we would be together, and we are, so what now?"

She deliberately didn't acknowledge the threats in his last letter. Her abductor sat down opposite her, staring at her with those unnaturally blue eyes, but saying nothing. Stella tried again. "Look, I haven't seen your face. You could stop all this now, and just let me go. Or tell me what you want from me, and we can try to make it work." She hid her feeling of nausea at the thought of being intimate with this monster.

He lifted the voice modifier to his mouth. "You're lying. You don't want me. Please don't insult my intelligence."

Stella sighed. "Then…why am I here?"

"To die."

Stella kept her composure. "But why? What have I ever done to you?" She silently cursed as her voice broke. "Why did you have to kill Biba?"

"What do you care about her?"

"She was my friend."

He gave a sarcastic laugh. "The way you treated her was not as a friend."

So, he was known to them. "Do you care about Biba? Do you care that you murdered a sweet girl?"

"I enjoyed it."

Oh, dear God…he got up and switched on the television. "You need to see this."

Stella was startled to see Cosimo in front of a bank of journalists with the FBI agent alongside him and Lars. He looked exhausted and drawn. Stella saw the 'Recorded Earlier' logo in the corner of the screen. She tried to concentrate on what Cosimo was saying.

"Please, whoever you are...you've already killed one person. This has to end now. Bring Stella back to us, unharmed, and we'll do everything we can to get you the help you need."

"He's lying," her captor said.

Stella ignored him. God. Cosimo looked heartbroken and Stella felt guilty—he had obviously loved Biba very much.

She got angry. "Why are you showing me this? What did you hope to achieve?"

He said nothing and, frustrated, Stella stood. "Let me go. Now. This is madness."

She only had time to blink once before he was on her.

## CHAPTER TWENTY-ONE

Biba watched as Cosimo spoke to the press. Since her parents had visited, she had been on edge, close to breaking. Her body ached, and she felt a million years old. Being around other people was irritating to her—except for Cosimo. She wanted all of this to be over so that Stella was safe, and Biba didn't have to carry this guilt around with her. If only she and Stella hadn't bickered...Stella might have been at the fireworks that night, and Rich might be alive.

Cosimo was kept busy with the journalists and Biba slipped away into the lounge of the hotel. She called Reggie, wanting to hear her old friend's voice.

"Hey, Boo."

"Hey, Reggie...how are you? How's Mary?"

"I'm good... but Mom's in a sugar coma."

Biba laughed, her body relaxing. "Seriously, how's the pneumonia?"

Reggie sighed. "It's not good, but you know Mom; she's a fighter. Any news on Stella?"

"None."

"I saw the press conference...not sure it'll do any good."

"No, neither are we, but we all feel so helpless, Reg. We just have no idea what the hell to do. If he asked for a ransom, that would be something, but it's like they've disappeared into thin air. She could be dead already..." Her voice quivered, and she began to cry softly.

"Oh, baby." Reggie's voice was soft. "Don't cry."

"I never knew I loved her until now," Biba sobbed. "She's a pain in the ass, but I love her like she's my sister. I can't bear to think of her scared and alone. Who knows what the asshole is doing to her. Stella's not as tough as she makes out."

There was a long silence on the end of the phone. "Darling... I know you. You're blaming yourself, and that isn't fair. How were you to know?"

"I could have fought harder."

"He stabbed you, Biba...no one could have fought harder."

Biba couldn't stop her tears. "Reg..."

"Look...do you want to come here? For a few days? To get away from everything?"

Suddenly, that's all she wanted to do. "I'll talk to Cos."

"I can come get you whenever."

While Biba didn't want to be away from Cosimo, she wanted to get away from Tacoma, and Cosimo agreed with her. "I want you out of danger, baby. I trust Reggie to keep you safe while we work all of this out."

They were alone in their hotel suite, late in the evening after a day of press and being around other people; they were both glad of the alone time. Cosimo stroked her face. "You look as if you're in pain."

"A little. The doctor said it would be painful as I healed. I just wish...I want to be close to you, Cosimo, especially now, and I feel as if my body is stopping that."

Cosimo kissed her. "You know, there's plenty of stuff we can do that won't strain your wounds."

Biba smiled. "Show me."

He undressed her slowly, kissing every piece of exposed skin, his lips tender against her body. His strong fingers stroked the length of her body, brushing over her nipples, making them stiffen and become so sensitive that she could hardly bear it.

Cosimo gently pressed her legs apart, moving down her body to take her clit into his mouth. Biba moaned softly as delicious sensations flooded her senses—this man was an expert, there was no doubt about it. He teased and lashed his tongue around the sensitive bud until she cried out, coming hard, her body shivering through it. A grinning Cosimo moved up to kiss her mouth. "See?"

Biba, a fine sheen of dewy sweat on her face, nodded. "My turn to please you."

She reached down to take his huge, throbbing cock into her hands and stroked the hot length of it against her thighs. One hand massaged his balls as she moved her other hand up and down his shaft, increasing the pressure and the speed until Cosimo gave a groan, and his cock shuddered and pumped hot, sticky semen onto her skin. They kissed passionately, both wanting more but knowing they couldn't risk it.

They caressed and explored each other's bodies for hours until, utterly exhausted, they fell asleep. In the morning, they were awoken by an excited Lars, telling them the FBI had a lead.

## CHAPTER TWENTY-TWO

They all sat in the hotel's conference room, listening to the FBI agent's radio communication on a sound system they had set up for them to hear the operation. Biba sat with Cosimo, her hand clutching his, her heart beating wildly in her chest. To know that soon, maybe, they'd get Stella back was making her feel sick with hope.

Please, please let her be okay...Biba swore to all her Gods that if they brought Stella back, she'd never argue with her again. Both of them would be changed by this, but she was determined that they would be changed for the better—both of them.

Luke Harris nodded to them as he came into the room. "Any minute now, you'll hear the lead getting his men into position."

"Where are they?"

"Rainier—a cabin near the Nisqually entrance to the park."

Biba studied the agent. If he brought Stella back safely, she would take back every negative thought she'd ever had about him. "How did you find them?"

"It's important to say that we haven't found them, we're just working on a tip. I don't want to give false hope, but this is the best lead we've had."

"From a tip?"

"An anonymous call from someone staying on the mountain. He told us he'd seen something suspicious—a woman fighting with a man—outside one of the cabins the night Ms. Reckless was taken."

"And it took him this long to call?" Cosimo's voice held all the skepticism that Biba felt. Luke Harris shrugged, and Biba tried not to snap at him. He really was the worst.

"So, the caller might have lied? The caller could have been the real killer throwing you off the scent?" Biba's voice was cold, but again Harris shrugged off her question.

"We don't think that's the case," he said, a smug, patronizing smile on his face. Biba wanted to punch him. Instead she leaned over to Cosimo and whispered in his ear.

"This isn't going to be what he thinks. I don't believe this is genuine."

Cosimo studied her. "I hope you're wrong, but I agree. Something is hinky."

As they waited to hear what happened, there was a knock at the door, and Reggie stuck his head in. "Can I join?"

"Of course."

He gave Biba a hug, clapped Cosimo on the back. "How goes it? Channing told me downstairs they've got a lead."

Biba shot him a look. "Yeah. Agent Harris is sure."

Reggie got her drift right away. "Ah."

Ten minutes later, Biba's worst fears were confirmed. The tip turned out to be a false alarm—the SWAT team burst in on a very shocked elderly couple who were doing a puzzle. Agent Harris looked crestfallen. "Well, obviously, we'll..."

But Biba had had enough. She got up and stalked out of the

conference room, followed by Cosimo and Reggie. Biba was steaming angry as she slammed into her suite.

"That asshole," she spat out, "he's not taking this seriously. This is Stella's life we're talking about."

Cosimo put his arms around her. "I know, Snooks." He looked at Reggie. "Look, Reg, I know you're here to take Biba to your mom's, but I want you to take protection with you."

"No problem," Reggie said, his eyes serious. "Anything to make sure Biba's safe."

Biba looked up at Cosimo. "I don't know if I want to go. No disrespect, Reg, but I need to stay with Cosimo."

"No," Cosimo said firmly. "You need to be away from all of this, so you can recover. I want to stick around, but I'll follow you up in a couple of days—if that's okay, Reg?"

"Perfect. Mom's cabin has plenty of room, so we'll have quite the party."

Cosimo smiled. "Thanks. So, baby, we won't be apart for long."

Biba wasn't happy but nodded. "Okay."

Cosimo went to seek out Steve, the head of his security, and asked him to accompany Biba and Reg. "Just don't let anything happen to them," he asked, and Steve nodded.

"I won't."

"And call me every hour to give me an update...okay?"

"Done and done, boss."

Before Biba left with Reggie, she and Cosimo took some private time. Pressing her lips to his, Biba kissed him, murmuring, "I love you so much, Cosimo DeLuca."

"Marry me, Biba May." Cosimo stroked her hair back from

her face. "I know it's crazy. I know we have so much to learn about each other, but I don't want to wait any longer. When all this is over, when Stella is safely back with us, marry me."

"Yes," Biba said without hesitation, "yes, my darling Cosimo, I will marry you. You're right. Let's not wait any longer."

Cosimo smiled, and it lit up his entire face. "I can't wait to be your husband."

"Nor I, your wife." She hesitated a little. "Do you think Nicco would mind?"

"Let's call him and ask."

Facetiming with him, they could tell Nicco was overjoyed. "Nice work, Pa," he said making Biba laugh. "I don't have to call you Mom, do I?"

"Hell, no," Biba made a face, "How about we just be besties?"

"I like that. So, when's the big day?"

"Unclear yet. When all this nightmare is cleared up, Nic." Cosimo smiled at his son.

"I'd like to get married in Venice," Biba said suddenly, "In the summer, all four of us together. Or five if we include Reggie—I'll need a bride's... man."

They all laughed, and Cosimo looked touched. "Then Venice it is..."

He kissed Biba and Nicco protested. "God, get a room."

As Reggie brought his car around and chatted with Steve, Cosimo kissed Biba goodbye. "I'll be happier knowing you're out of the line of fire. I love you."

On the journey to Reggie's mom's cabin in the Olympic mountains, they chatted about nothing in particular, aware of Steve's presence in the car behind them.

"I just wish this was all over," Biba said, "I keep thinking how scared Stella must be."

"Don't think about it," Reggie said, "I'll bet your imaginings are worse than the reality."

Biba frowned. "Dude, did you read the crap he sent her? Guy's a nutjob."

"I know that, but what I'm saying is, maybe once he actually got her, he chickened out."

"Chickened out? Reg...this man stabbed Rich seven times. He stabbed me twice. I doubt chickening out is in his wheelhouse." She was mad now, staggered by her best friend's lack of sensitivity.

"I don't want to argue, bugs."

They drove on in an uncomfortable silence for a while, Biba wondering if she had made the right decision. Now, driving away from Cosimo, she felt more vulnerable, not less.

As they entered the Olympics, Reg suddenly looked at his gauges. "Shit."

Her attention was caught. "What is it?" She noticed the car slowing. Outside, the snow was coming down heavily as Reg put the blinkers on and moved to the side if the road.

"Car's misbehaving. Hang on..."

He stopped the vehicle and got out, walking to the front and popping the hood. Biba looked around and saw Steve pull up behind them. He got out of the car and walked around their car. He knocked on her window, mouthing, "You okay?" Biba nodded and gave him the thumbs up, and Steve continued around to talk to Reggie.

Biba waited while the two men took a look at the car, jumping slightly when the hood was slammed back down. Biba watched them talk, but then as Steve turned away, everything changed.

In horror, Biba watched as Reggie pulled a handgun from his jacket and leveled it at the back of Steve's head. "No!" Biba screamed, but it was too late.

Reggie shot Steve in the head, and the bodyguard dropped like a stone. Biba couldn't believe what she was seeing. She clawed at the door of the car and staggered out, staring at her best friend.

Reggie smiled at her. "Don't run, Biba. I don't want to kill you here."

Her legs wouldn't move even though every cell in her body told her to run. Reggie was at her side in a flash, taking her upper arm and dragging her back to the car. He pressed the gun to her wounded belly, hard, and she gasped at the pain. "Now, in the glove compartment, you'll find some handcuffs. I want you to cuff your left hand and put it around the back of your seat. Try anything and I'll empty this whole clip into you."

Was this really happening? Her best friend? Her Reggie? Had he gone crazy?

Biba did as she was told, and Reggie cuffed her right hand to her left. She was trapped.

Reggie got back in the driver's seat. "Now, let's go. I know someone is looking forward to seeing you."

## CHAPTER TWENTY-THREE

Cosimo couldn't shake the feeling that something was terribly wrong. He sought out Lars, who was working at one of the tables in the lounge. Lars smiled at him as he sat down.

"Biba get away okay?"

Cosimo nodded. "Fine, but now I'm thinking I shouldn't have let her out of my sight."

"It's the yips," Lars said with a shrug. "We've all got them since Stella. She's with Reggie and Steve, Cos, they'll die before they let anything happen to her."

Cosimo sighed. "You're right. Any news?"

"Not on Stella, but Rich's family is suing the studio."

"Well, I don't blame them. Tell them I'll support them in their bid."

"They're suing you, too," Lars said with a half-laugh, and Cosimo snorted.

"I don't blame them for that either. Tell their lawyer I'll settle."

"Seventeen million?"

"Do it."

Lars laughed again. "Oh, to be a billionaire."

Cosimo smiled, but his eyes were serious. "I'm responsible, Lars. When I'm the director on a film set and something like this happens, I'm responsible. I should have upped the security, asked for a different FBI agent—so much more."

"Dude, you had an army—relatively speaking, of course."

Cosimo rubbed his face then pulled his cell phone out of his pocket. "Steve's supposed to be checking in every hour."

"How long ago did they leave?"

"Forty minutes."

Lars took the phone from Cosimo. "You'll drive yourself crazy like that. C'mon, man, relax a little. There's nothing else to do."

"Maybe I should follow them up to the cabin."

"Jesus, Cos." Sifrido came up behind them, rolling his eyes. "Always the control freak. Relax, brother."

He flopped down into an easy chair and exchanged a look with Lars that Cosimo didn't understand. Lars picked up his phone. "Gotta make a call. Be right back."

Cosimo waited until Lars had left and then looked at Sifrido. "What is it?"

Sifrido hesitated. "I'm not sure this is the right time to bring this up. Then again, I don't think there is a good time to have this conversation."

"Just spill it, 'Frido."

Sifrido squared his shoulders and nodded. "It's about Grace...and me. And one night sixteen years ago."

He didn't need to say anymore, but Cosimo would bet all of his money he wasn't expecting the reaction Cosimo gave him. "Oh, thank God."

Sifrido's eyebrows shot up. "What?"

Cosimo started to laugh. "As weird as this sounds...I'm glad. I'm glad it's you, 'Frido. I had always suspected you and Grace were attracted to each other, I just didn't know you'd acted on it. But, God, I'm relieved. Knowing Nicco...you know."

Sifrido was incredulous. "You're okay with raising another man's son?"

Cosimo smiled. "I did no such thing. I raised my son. Nicco is my child regardless of whose DNA he shares. If these past few weeks has taught me anything, it's that family doesn't mean sharing blood. It's more profound than that. You are my family, 'Frido, so the fact you and Grace...I don't care. Nicco is my son, and I love him more than anything."

"Apart from Biba?"

"On par with Biba. I'm not saying finding out he wasn't my biological son wasn't a shock, but by God, 'Frido, I could not be prouder of Nicco and the man he's becoming."

Sifrido ran his hand through his hair, still not believing what was happening. "I'm sorry about Grace. It was a moment of weakness, and we both felt awful afterward. I don't think she knew about Nicco. I truly believe she thought Nicco was yours."

Cosimo got up and hugged his friend. "Do you want to tell Nicco?"

"I don't know. Would he rather not know?"

Cosimo pondered the question. "I'll ask him."


HE CALLED Nicco a little while later and told him that he found out who his father was.

"Yeah, you," said Nicco, "but I suppose I should know whose DNA I got."

Cosimo was relieved when Nicco took the news well. "Better than expected," Nicco said, "at least 'Frido's a friend."

"That's what I said."

"Although I will have to pound on him just a little bit for messing with my mom."

Cosimo chuckled, knowing Nicco was joking. "I guess that's your prerogative."

"How's Biba?"

Immediately the weight in Cosimo's chest returned. "On her way to Reggie's mom's cabin." He checked his watch. "And her protection is late calling in. Nic, I have to go."

"Sure, Dad. Give Beebs my love."

"I will."

Cosimo ended the call and dialed Steve's cell phone. Even if he were driving, Steve should have hands-free, but the phone rang and rang. After ten rings, it went to voicemail.

It's okay, don't panic, everything is okay. He sucked in a deep breath, telling himself to relax.

AFTER THREE HOURS, however, he knew. Something was terribly wrong. He went to find Lars and Channing. "Guys," he said in a grim voice. "I'm calling the police. Both of you—get on the phones and find out everything you can about Reggie Quinn. I think our killer was hiding in plain sight all this time."

## CHAPTER TWENTY-FOUR

Reggie shoved Biba, still cuffed, into the cabin, and she whimpered when she saw Mary Quinn's body propped up in the chair. "God, what did you do?" Her whisper was full of grief. Mary? There was no doubt what had happened to her seeing the gaping hole in her neck.

Reggie smiled. "Momma's at peace now. She was really sick, Biba."

Her eyes narrowed. "Like her son."

He laughed. "Being in love isn't a sickness, Biba, you should know that. My love for Stella is real, a dream, and now you are going to help that dream come true."

He undid her cuffs but kept a tight hold on her as he steered her towards the back of the cabin. Unlocking a door, he pushed her inside.

Biba saw Stella at the same time her boss saw her. Stella gave a cry, and the two women threw themselves at each other, embracing hard. "I thought you were dead. I thought you were dead," was all Stella could say through hysterical sobs.

Biba held her so hard she could feel her arms going numb. "It's okay, it's okay now, I'm here."

"How sweet."

Stella rounded on Reggie. "You told me you killed her."

Reggie shrugged. "Semantics. It'll be true soon."

Biba couldn't believe what was happening. Reggie? Her person? Her best friend? "You stabbed me."

He smiled. "I did. I hadn't planned on hurting anybody, but first Rich, then you got in my way."

"He told me he enjoyed stabbing you." Stella was holding Biba's hand. "Didn't you, you sick fuck?"

Reggie laughed. "I did, I admit it. And it was true, sinking my knife into your soft belly, Biba, I got hard. Which is why I'm going to do it again, only this time, there won't be a happy ending for you."

"Don't you touch her!" Stella dragged Biba behind her. Biba was just numb.

"Why do you think I brought her here, Stella? She's our insurance. We'll make it to the Canadian border with her, then I'll stab her to death and leave her body somewhere to throw the feds off the scent. We'll be in the wind before they know it. Plus, while she's with us, Cosimo will do anything I tell him to."

Biba didn't even feel afraid. Reggie was going to kill her. He was going to use her murder to help him escape with Stella, and to torment Cosimo. Bastard. She had no intention of going quietly.

"You'll have to kill me first," Stella growled at him, but Biba shook her head.

"He won't do it. He hasn't got the guts." She faced down her old friend, the man she had thought for such a long time was the only person she could trust.

Reggie studied her. "You know, you've changed since you started fucking DeLuca. I have to admit, I was surprised. For years, you were telling me about how you were abused as a kid, how sex wasn't important, how you'd never trust a man. That you were broken inside. Then the handsome rich Italian turns up, and you open your legs as wide as they will go."

"Fuck. You." Biba said, ignoring Stella's whimper of fear. "You have no idea what real love is. It's not this. Keeping someone prisoner, threatening them, aggression. So, who's the dysfunctional one out of the two of us, Reg?"

"I'm going to enjoy killing you, Biba."

"You're not going to get the chance, asshole. Now, you want to go right now, because I'm in the mood to kick your ass into next Tuesday."

Reggie laughed mirthlessly and then grabbed her, twisting his fingers in her hair as he held the knife to her throat. Biba stamped on his instep, ignoring the knife. Reggie roared with pain and released her, but he still managed to lash out with his knife, slicing through her back just above her buttock. Biba gasped, Stella screamed, and Reggie slammed his elbow into Biba's head, and everything went dark.

For once, Agent Luke Harris wasn't being cocky. "We have men on the way to the cabin now, but there's a pretty bad storm going on up there. We can't fly in."

"No. No, you get there however you can as fast as you can," Cosimo was yelling, his terror making him almost wild. "He's going to kill both of them."

Sifrido, Lars, Channing, and Franco were equally worried. "Look, if you won't send people out, we'll go," Sifrido said. Harris held up his hands.

"No, you're not listening. We are sending people out, lots of them, but I cannot control the weather. We send choppers up there, they will crash. More people will die. I swear to you all—

we have an army headed up to the Olympics. Quinn won't get far."

Cosimo ran his hands through his dark curls and closed his eyes. "I gave her to him."

"How the hell would you know any different? Reggie fooled us all."

Franco nodded. "And look...we still don't know for sure that anything is wrong. It could be the storm's taken out Steve's cell service."

For an hour or so, Cosimo kept that in his mind to stop himself from going crazy. But his resolve was shattered when a pale, stricken-looking Harris caught up with them. "We found Steve Kimmel's body. He was shot in the head, and Reggie's car is gone."

Cosimo put his head in his hands, and when Harris left them to go get an update, he looked up into Sifrido's concerned face. "I need to get there, 'Frido. I need to save her... them."

Sifrido hesitated for one second. "My car is outside. Let's go."

## CHAPTER TWENTY-FIVE

Biba woke, feeling woozy and nauseous. Stella was cradling her head in her lap. "Biba?" Her voice was a whisper. Biba realized they were in a vehicle, moving.

"Where are we?"

"Going towards Canada, I think. I'm not sure. No, don't move too much. That cut on your back is bleeding like crazy; I can't get it to stop."

Shit. That meant the slash of the knife had gone too deep, probably nicked a kidney. She was bleeding to death—slowly. Biba swallowed a throatful of vomit.

"Stella...get closer."

Stella bent her head to Biba's, and Biba felt Stella's tears on her cheek. "Don't cry, Stel. I'm going to get you out of here."

Stella gave a strange laugh. "Beebs, you can't even walk."

"I can...just. I'm going to go for Reggie and get him to steer off the road. I want you to hang on in here as hard as you can. The moment we come to a stop, you get out and you run. Don't stop, just get as far as you can...flag down a car."

"You're delirious, baby. You can't make it. We won't make it."

"It's our only chance."

"He has a gun…he'll shoot you."

Biba laughed softly. "I'm dying, anyway. The least I can do is go out in a blaze of glory."

Stella buried her face in Biba's shoulder and sobbed. "I'm so sorry for the way I've treated you, Biba…the truth is, you're the only person in this world who I trust, and one of the few I truly love. You've always had my back. Always. But I can't leave you here to die for me. Not going to happen. We do this together or not at all."

"Girl power." Biba's voice was weakening.

"You bet your ass. And—"

Her words were cut off as the van lurched to a stop, and Reggie got out. They heard him unlock the back doors. They'd run out of time.

"Pretend I'm dead," Biba whispered urgently. "Scream, make a fuss. It'll give me time."

Stella nodded, and let out an ear-piercing scream. Biba tried not to flinch as her eardrums protested. A rush of freezing cold air.

"She's dead, you bastard! Biba's dead! She fucking bled to death while you…Jesus, what the hell is wrong with you?"

There was a silence. Biba could only hear Stella's heavy breathing. Then… "She's dead?"

Faint hope ignited inside Biba—Reggie sounded shocked, even a little heartbroken.

"Well, Goddamn, he catches up," Stella said, sarcastically, cradling Biba's head in her arms. "She was your best friend, Reggie, and you killed her. How does that make you feel, huh?"

Then Reggie chuckled, and Biba's hope dissolved. "Well, I guess it saves me killing her later. Leave her body. They're following us; they'll find her. Wish I could stay to see DeLuca's face."

"No." Biba's whisper was urgent. "Don't let him take you."

"I'm not going anywhere without her."

Biba felt Stella being dragged away from her. No... no... As she heard Reggie's voice growing distant, she hauled herself up, her clothes sticky with blood. She limped to the van's driver's seat, hunting for anything she could use as a weapon. Underneath the passenger's seat, she found a tire iron. Better than nothing. Ignoring the searing pain in her back, Biba staggered out into the storm to follow Reggie and Stella.

COSIMO AND SIFRIDO drove in silence, both on edge as the storm grew worse around them. Two hours into the park, and they saw the van on the side of the road. "Where the hell are the FBI, if we can find this?"

"It might not be anything," Sifrido cautioned as they got out of the car, but when they inspected the van, Cosimo saw the back of it awash with blood, and on the floor: a small charm bracelet. He reached in and picked up the delicate gold chain with the single diamond hanging from it.

"It's them," he said in a dull voice. "I gave this to Biba for her birthday."

Sifrido patted his shoulder. "I think they went this way."

Cosimo didn't move. "'Frido, look at all this blood. Someone bled out here."

"Not necessarily...Cos, there's a blood trail here. C'mon."

THEY FOUND BIBA, slumped over in the snow, barely conscious. Cosimo scooped her into his arms and held her close while Sifrido examined her wounds.

"Jesus, it's deep. We need to get her back to civilization."

"No," Biba moaned, "we're so close. They're just ahead of me. Please, save her... For me, Cos, save her."

Cosimo hesitated, and Biba touched his face. "This will all have been for nothing if we don't." She wriggled out of his arms and stood as best she could. "I'm okay, I think." She saw the skepticism in her face and tried to smile. "Okay, I'm not, but fuck it, he isn't going to win."

"Then hold onto me and do not let go," Cosimo said, sliding his arm around her waist. "If we're going to do this, we're going to do it together." They set off slowly along the tracks Reggie and Stella had left.

"He has a gun. Just thought I'd mention it." The blood loss was making her lightheaded and squirrelly. Cosimo almost smiled.

"Always helpful to know."

Ten minutes later, Sifrido stopped them, putting his finger to his lips and pointing downhill. They saw flashes of color amidst the snowy trees and heard a woman's voice carrying back to them.

"Stella's giving him hell," Biba whispered, and Cosimo nodded.

"If he thinks that's hell, he's about to find out what hell is really like." He lowered her to the ground, propped up against a tree. "Baby, we need to take him by surprise, and as much as I love you, we can't do that holding you up."

Biba nodded. "I get it."

"I'm going to be back before you know it." He pressed his lips to his. "My little warrior. I love you."

"Love you too...be careful." Biba smiled at him, then her eyes lit up. "I have a weapon." She pulled the tire iron from her pocket. Cosimo stroked her face.

"You hang onto that, just in case. We brought our own." He

showed her the guns he and Sifrido had brought with them. Biba nodded.

"Kill that motherfucker. He murdered Rich and his own mother."

Cosimo nodded, his eyes dangerous. "Don't worry...Reggie Quinn is going down."

## CHAPTER TWENTY-SIX

Stella struggled with Reggie, no longer concerned about herself. She was just determined that if she was killed, she was taking this asshole with her. "You piece of shit, you left her to die."

"I thought you told me she was dead." Reggie was smirking. His fingers were tangled in Stella's blonde hair, dragging her down the hill.

"Motherfucker!" She kicked out and caught him on the knee. Reggie buckled and dragged her down with him as he fell.

"You fucking bitch!" He hit her hard, making her ears ring, but then she heard it. A gunshot.

Hope.

She looked up and saw two very angry Italian men bearing down on them. Cosimo levelled his gun at Reggie. "Time's up, Quinn."

"Fuck you, DeLuca."

Reggie attempted to grab Stella to hold his own gun to her head, but Stella had really had enough. With the heel of her hand, she slammed it into his nose. With a screech, Reggie dropped the gun, his nose pouring with blood. Stella kicked him away from her and scrambled in the snow to get away. Cosimo scooped her up as Sifrido aimed his gun at Reggie's face.

"Due process?" He asked Cosimo and Stella.

"Rich didn't get due process."

"Or this scumbag's mother!" Stella spat. Sifrido smiled grimly.

Reggie started to laugh. "Nor your precious Biba. I enjoyed slicing her up, DeLuca. I really, really enjoyed it."

Sifrido shot him in the face, and Reggie dropped. Calmly, Sifrido wrapped Reggie's fingers around his own gun and fired it into the trees. "Cos, go walk around over there, make it look like he was firing at you."

Cosimo did as he asked and then they left Reggie's body for the FBI to find. The three of them hurried back to Biba who smiled at all of them. "I love you all," she said, sounding drunk. "Is he dead?"

"As a dodo." Cosimo lifted her into his arms. Stella smoothed Biba's hair away from her face.

"Love you, Beebs." She ignored Cosimo and Sifrido's astonished glances, but Biba saw them and grinned.

"You boys never see some lady love? Love you, too, Stel. Now, can I ask a question?"

"Anything, baby." Cosimo kissed her forehead.

Biba smiled. "Anyone mind if I pass out now?"

## CHAPTER TWENTY-SEVEN

Four months later...

STELLA TOUCHED FRANCO'S FACE. "Thornton, after everything we've been through—the horror, the torment—surely now you know that I have loved you from the very beginning."

"Thornton" nodded. "My darling Lucy...I just wish it hadn't taken your death to convince me...I wish I could have saved you, my love, my precious love."

"We will be together soon, my darling...I am waiting for you...I am waiting..."

"AND CUT! That's a wrap, folks! Congrats and thank you all." Cosimo led the applause as the cast and crew finally relaxed. They had been back on set for a month finishing up the movie, and everyone had returned, all determined to finish what they started. The film would be dedicated to Rich

Furlough—to Cosimo that was a no-brainer, but he also wanted to honor Biba, too. It had been Stella's idea to start up a foundation to provide opportunities within the movie industry for young people. The Biba May Foundation for the Arts, Stella had declared, as they had sat in Biba's hospital room, talking and recovering from the terrible events of the past few months.

Biba had objected at the name. "I really don't think it should be named after me. Who am I?"

Cosimo had opened his mouth, but Stella had beaten him to it. "You're the heroine who saved me. You put yourself in danger multiple times to save my life—and yes, Cos and 'Frido had a huge part to play, too, but Beebs, do you know the inspiration you are to young women everywhere?"

"I agree. The Biba May Foundation for the Arts, and that's final. And I'll personally put ten million in to start." Cosimo nodded, pleased.

"I'll match it."

Biba had watched as Cosimo and Stella had gotten more and more excited over their plans and wondered about how her life had turned out. Her boss was now her best friend, and her employer was her lover. And she loved these two people more than anyone.

She had spent months recovering from her physical wounds— to her relief, her kidney hadn't been badly damaged by Reggie's knife, but the psychological horror of Reggie's betrayal, of his years of lies and manipulation, had left her depressed and at times, inconsolable.

With the exception of Cosimo and Stella, Biba had lost the person she trusted most, and even though she was glad he was gone, she missed having that comfort. She hated feeling like that and had slumped into a depression that even Cosimo had trouble rousing her from.

Now, though, she was making it out onto the other side. Watching her lover finally finish the film they had all come to Lakewood to make, seeing the relief on his handsome face was exhilarating. Cosimo came over to her and took her in his arms.

"We did it, Snooks." His eyes were shining, and Biba smiled.

"We did. Congratulations, baby."

Cosimo pressed his lips against hers. "I love you, Miss May."

Biba wrapped her arms around his neck, not caring about the others who were chuckling and watching. "I love you too, Mr. DeLuca."

They kissed passionately until the others started to catcall them, making them laugh. Stella came up to them. "Listen you two, we're having a wrap party this evening, and we have a little surprise waiting for you."

Cosimo grinned, and Biba's eyebrows shot up. "You do?"

Stella hugged her. "A good surprise, I promise. Until then… there's a suite up there that needs to be used."

"Pimp."

"You know it." Stella grinned at them both then went back to talking to Franco, Sifrido, and the crew. The change in her attitude since the abduction was still astonishing to everyone. Stella was laid back, inclusive, friendly, and warm.

"The weird thing was," Biba said now as she and Cosimo made their way back to the manor, "is that I believe that was always the real Stella, anyway. That the diva thing was a way of protecting herself."

"I think you may be right," Cosimo said and grinned down at her. "But then you always saw the best in everyone."

Biba's smile faded a little, and Cosimo stopped her with a

hand on her shoulder. "Biba, he fooled us all. Reggie Quinn had all the appearance of goodness. Don't blame yourself for him."

I*N THEIR SUITE*, they undressed each other slowly, kissing every piece of exposed skin until they were both shivering with desire.

"The bed," Cosimo said with a grin, and Biba, laughing, wiggled her eyebrows.

"On the floor, baby." She shrieked with laughter as Cosimo wrestled her playfully to the floor and covered her body with his. Cosimo himself had seemed more fun-loving since the horror of her injuries had faded, eager to enjoy every moment of their time together. In a couple of days, they would be flying to Italy to visit his hometown of Venice and plan their wedding. Biba couldn't wait to go, to get away from the States for a few weeks.

Stella had insisted Biba take a few months off.

"Full pay, of course, and there'll be a bonus as well. Just hang with Cos, relax, chill, plan the wedding. When you're ready to come back, we should talk about you being my manager, not my assistant. You're too good for that, and I've known it for years."

S*O*, now, relaxing with Cosimo, making love slowly and leisurely, Biba should have felt the happiest she'd ever been. Cosimo was trailing his lips against her jaw, pressing them against her throat, working his way all the way down her body. Biba wriggled with pleasure and moaned as his tongue touched her clit. "God, Cos…yes. Yes…that's it…God…"

Cosimo took his time, lashing his tongue around her clit then burying it deep into her cunt until she was gasping his name and coming hard, arching her back, and when he plunged his cock inside her, she came again, shivering and shuddering.

And she was happy except...something was missing. Something was unresolved, and now as they relaxed together, wrapping their arms around each other, she talked to Cosimo about how she was feeling.

"What do you think it is?" Cosimo asked her, stroking her cheek. Biba shook his head.

"I honestly don't know, baby. I'm sure the feeling will fade."

BUT EVEN AS they made their way back to their friends, that evening, Biba felt it—something was unfinished. Yes, that was it, she needed closure on...what? What was it?

Soon, though, her attention was taken by the lakeside gathering as they lit Chinese lanterns and set them onto the water. "Oh, this is gorgeous," Biba said, and Cosimo smiled.

"I'm glad you think so, Biba May. Come with me."

He led her out onto the tiny jetty where they had almost made love for the first time. Biba chuckled. "Dude, there's like a hundred people watching us, so if you're hoping for a do-over..."

Cosimo laughed, his green eyes dancing. "No, this isn't that...for now. But, Biba, Stella helped me organize this little soiree, because there's a very important question I need to ask you."

Warmth flooded her system. Emotion rushing up her body as Cosimo knelt in front of her. "Biba May, my darling love, you have changed my life. You are my heroine, my savior, my very best friend. Would you do me the great honor of becoming my wife?"

Biba, tears in her eyes, grinned. "You bet your sweet Italian ass I will!"

Cosimo burst out laughing. "And there was me being all formal. So, it's a yes?"

Biba threw her arms around his neck. "Yes, yes, yes!" Cosimo picked her up and swung her around, and Biba heard their friends cheering, obviously guessing her answer.

Cosimo put her down finally, tears glistening on his long lashes. "I love you so much, Biba May. You are the love of my life."

Biba was shocked into silence, for a few seconds. "I am?"

Cosimo nodded. "That's not to say I didn't love Grace with all my heart, I did. But, Biba, I didn't think my heart could take another risk, and yet you made it impossible not to. I love you."

Biba was crying now, and she buried her face in his chest. "I love you, too, Cosimo DeLuca."

He kissed her softly. "Come on, baby. Let's go see our friends and celebrate with them."


AT THE AIRPORT, Nicco and Olivia joined them. "I'm definitely gonna call you the evil stepmom," Nicco grinned at Biba, who punched his arm, laughing.

"And you're the evil spawn stepson."

"That's my job."

Cosimo and Biba both rolled their eyes. "Flight's delayed for an hour, so we might as well grab something to eat."

In the restaurant, Nicco fell on his burger. "So, Pa, why aren't we taking the private jet?"

Cosimo grinned at Biba. "Because of the environment, Nicco."

"Glad to hear it." Nicco exchanged a look with his grandmother. "By the way, I have news."

"Go for it."

Nicco grinned. "I have early acceptance at Oregon State."

Cosimo looked taken aback, then delighted. "Damn, Nicco... wow! God, I don't know what to say. Congratulations, son."

"Thanks, Dad, and I know you wanted me to consider Stanford, and I swear to you, I did. Me and G-Ma went to the campus a week or so ago, and it's beautiful...but I need my pine forests and rain."

"Word." Biba tapped her soda glass to his, and he winked at her.

"Thanks, Beebs. So, Dad?"

Cosimo got up and hugged Nicco. "I could not be prouder. You killed it with that 4.0."

"Oh, I know," Nicco was all swagger as he sat back down.

"You didn't want to take a gap year?"

Nicco shook his head. "Nah, I want to get on with it, you know? I'll do the years of under- and post-grad. I cannot wait to get to do the actual work. And I've broadened my scope, too. Ever since we went to Rainier, I can't stop thinking about specializing in volcanology, both on land and under the sea."

Cosimo was shaking his head, smiling. "What happened to my sulky teen?"

They chatted for a little while more, and then decided to walk to the departure gate. Biba held Cosimo's hand as Nicco and Olivia walked in front of them. She stopped suddenly and looked at Cosimo with nervous eyes. "Baby... I need to make a call."

Cosimo looked concerned. "Everything okay?"

"Oh yes," she said, and gave him a smile. "I just figured out the unfinished business."

She could tell from the way his eyes shone at her that he knew what she was talking about. "You want some privacy?"

She shook her hand. "No, I need you to hold my hand."

"For the rest of our lives," he said softly, "you can count on that."

Nicco and Olivia looked back at them, somehow knowing

this was a moment that wasn't to be shared. They moved away to a discreet distance as Biba took out her phone. She scrolled to the number she wanted, then hesitated, her finger hovering over the screen.

"No matter what," Cosimo said softly, "you are loved beyond words."

Tears in her eyes, Biba kissed him, then pressed the call button. When the call was accepted, she drew in a long shaky breath.

"Mom," she said, finally, "It's me. It's Biba..."

**THE END**

# SIGN UP TO RECEIVE FREE BOOKS

**Sign Up to Receive Free E-Books and Audiobook Codes.**

Would you like to read **The Unexpected Nanny, Dirty Little Virgin** and **other romance books** for **free**?

You can sign up to receive these free e-books and audiobooks by typing this link into your browser:

https://www.steamyromance.info/free-books-and-audiobooks-hot-and-steamy/

Or this one:

https://www.steamyromance.info/the-unexpected-nanny-free/

# PREVIEW OF DARK MASQUERADE

A Bad Boy Billionaire Romance

By Michelle Love

### Blurb

When award-winning writer Elliana Moretti is hired by billionaire philanthropist Aldo Costanza to write his biography, she travels to his secluded mansion outside Venice to interview him. Over the course of six weeks of intensive one-on-one collaborations, an attraction between them emerges, and one night, that attraction develops into a full-blown fling, erotic and intense. The night leaves Elli feeling as if she has been unprofessional and she tells Aldo that while she enjoyed the night, it can never happen again.

Aldo accepts this with seeming good grace, but one night, he asks her to escort him to a society party, where she is stunned to meet an old friend, Indio Navaro—her high school crush and noted bad boy billionaire. Indio and Aldo seem acquainted, if a little reserved with each other, and Elli wonders what the story is between them. Aldo is more than happy to trash Indio to Elli later that night, telling her that Indio was responsible for breaking up one of Aldo's relationships with a girl who later ended up murdered.

Elli is horrified, but Aldo's story doesn't seem to fit with how she remembers Indio from school.

Indio approaches Elli in a café in Venice, and curious, she agrees to have lunch with him. Elli's old crush is charming and appears genuinely interested in her. Elli begins to doubt Aldo's story.

Soon, she and Indio are spending more time together, to Aldo's great jealousy, and Elli finds herself giving her body, her trust, and her heart to Indio. But when Elli finds she is being stalked, she has to wonder whether Indio is indeed more dangerous that she could ever have expected. Has she fallen in love with a killer …or her savior?

Does she trust her client, Aldo, or does she follow her heart and believe Indio when he tells her that Aldo is the one she should be afraid of?

Set in the swirling, colorful romance of Venice's Carnival, Elli has to figure which one of her admirers plays the best game in an erotic but deadly Masquerade …

## 28

## VENICE, ITALY
DECEMBER

Elliana Moretti pulled her too-thin coat around her as she hurried over the bridges and through the small streets of Venice to work. An ice storm had blown through the city, and as usual, Elli had been completely unprepared for it.

At twenty-eight, Elli had made a name for herself as a tenacious investigative journalist, focused entirely on her career. Her beauty was useful, getting her through the door of places she might otherwise have been refused from, but once she had her prey on her hook, her intelligence and talent were what most people admired about her. Vivienne Marche, publishing maven, had seen those qualities when Elli had applied for an internship with her. Elli had worked for Vivienne for five years at their San Francisco office before they both relocated back to Elli's hometown to start the new magazine.

Today, the magazine, a women-led political and social monthly, was hosting a lunch for Aldo Costanza, an American-Italian philanthropist billionaire who had recently relocated to Venice from Rome. Vivienne had told Elli that the man was thinking of investing heavily in the magazine.

"It would mean the magazine could go international." Vivienne was excited. Elli could see that. "It would mean I could send my top journalist abroad to dig out the stories she really wants to write," Vivienne added, with a meaningful look at a grinning Elli.

"Well, in that case ..." Elli chuckled, enthused by her boss's excitement.

Now, as Elli walked briskly through the frozen Venice streets, she was trying to compile in her head a list of stories she had wanted to go deep into and the possibilities that lay ahead. She was so lost in thought that she didn't see the car as she walked across the road. Someone shouted a warning, and she looked up to see the car bearing down on her. She jumped back and slipped, crashing to the cold, hard ground and slamming her head against the stone. The car skimmed past her without stopping.

For a second, dazed, she lay there, head whirling, until she felt someone crouch down beside her. "Are you all right?"

Elli pushed herself into a sitting position, still stunned. A man peered down at her. "You're bleeding, Bella."

He pulled a clean, white handkerchief from his pocket and pressed it to her temple. "Should I call an ambulance?"

Elli was horrified and tried to get up. "No, I'm fine. Thank you for stopping to help me. It was just a fall ..." She swallowed hard when she saw the amount of blood on the man's handkerchief and her head whirled.

"Sweet one, I think we should go get you checked out anyway ...you might need stitches."

In one swift movement, he swept her up into his arms and was carrying her toward his huge, black Mercedes. Elli wanted to protest, but she couldn't form the words. God, her head was killing her ...damn, what if she'd cracked her skull? Today, of all days? Of anyone, Elli would hate to let Vivienne down; her boss was like her big sister as well as her mentor and her heroine.

The man put her in the back of his car and got in beside her, calling an order to his driver. He cradled her in his arms. Elli felt her body get cold—was she in shock? It was just a fall, goddamn it ...but her head whirled and she felt faint and nauseous. Her companion stroked her hair back from the wound.

"Sweetheart, you must stay awake for me. What's your name?"

"Elliana."

"A name as beautiful as its owner."

He had a nice voice, she thought fuzzily. But now there were black spots in her vision and her chest felt tight.

"Elliana, don't faint on me now ..."

His voice faded into the recesses of her memory as she slipped away into darkness.

Elli woke on a gurney in a hospital room. She blinked a couple of times and felt pain sear through her skull. She moaned quietly, then heard a scrape of a chair on linoleum.

"Elli? Welcome back."

Turning her head caused a jolt of pain that nearly drew the curtains back over her eyes once more.

"Stay still," the voice warned, coming closer until the face attached to it swam into view.

Elli squinted, making out dark hazel eyes, stubble, and light brown hair cropped close to his head. He looked vaguely familiar. Somewhere at the back of her battered brain, she also registered that he was seriously good looking, but it hurt too much to put that into any kind of context.

The man leaned down, bringing those warm eyes that much closer, and gently brushed her cheek with his knuckle. Heat flared through her for a moment, bright enough to dislodge the dizziness. "Stay still, Bella," he repeated softly. "You have a bad concussion."

"What happened?" she asked in confusion.

"You were very nearly hit by a car. It could have been far worse, but you have a severe concussion, Bella," he repeated. "They've stitched your head wound. You'll be okay, but you'll have to stay here for a day or two."

Elli sat up in horror, ignoring the pull of the I.V. tube in her arm. "No ...no, I can't. I have to work. I have to be there today." She could feel herself starting to panic, and he sat on the side of her bed and took her cold hand in his large, warm one. Again, there was a pulse of heat that moved through her body like a slow-burning flame.

"Sweet one, let me call your workplace—where do you work?"

. "Il Mondo Italia," she rasped. "We're a ..."

"Magazine, yes I know," he said, grinning. "I'm a subscriber."

"You are?"

He laughed. "Of course. And as you are Elliana, you must be Elliana Moretti. Your work is the reason I subscribe."

She gaped at him. "That's not true."

"Hand on my heart. Hi, Elliana Moretti ...I'm Aldo Constanza."


VIVIENNE MARCHE'S eyes grew huge as she saw her best friend and top journalist, Elli, complete with a bandage wrapped around her head and a bruised, pale face, being escorted into the magazine's offices by Aldo Constanza. Ordinarily, any unexpected appearance by Aldo would have been cause for scrambling in the office, but Vivienne presently had no interest in anything but her friend.

"Elli!" She jumped out of her seat and rushed around to carefully embrace the woman who she called sister. "What happened?"

Aldo greeted her warmly before Elli could say anything. "Vivienne, how wonderful to see you again. This little one insisted on bringing me today, despite her accident. Elli, please sit down before you fall down."

"Accident? What accident?" Vivienne demanded, easing Elli into a seat and hovering beside her.

"She only just missed being struck by a car," Aldo explained. "Her head took the brunt of her narrow escape."

"Why didn't you call me?" exclaimed Vivienne in horror, very nearly pulling Elli into a bearhug before realizing she might have other, unseen injuries. She contented herself instead with taking Elli's hand and holding onto it tightly.

Aldo nodded at the head bandage. "She was indisposed."

"The pavement has a dent in it," Elli joked wearily. "No major damage done to this hard head."

In spite of her attempt at lightheartedness, Vivienne could see the embarrassment in Elli's eyes. She pressed Elli's fingers as Aldo continued. "She has a severe concussion, and I think she should have gone straight home from the hospital, but she insisted on bringing me here."

Vivienne's heart warmed. That was just like Elli. She pressed her lips to Elli's temple. "You are a peach," she said. "But I'm sending you home right now, El. I'll arrange a cab."

"No, please. I insist my driver take her home." Aldo was firm, and so in a few minutes, Vivienne was tucking Elli into the warm backseat of Aldo Constanza's limousine, lingering worriedly in the door to admonish,

"You take as long as you need, El. I don't want you back until you're well."

Elli smiled gratefully at her. "I'm so sorry about this, Viv."

"Don't be silly." Vivienne leaned in closer, "If anything, you've broken the ice with Constanza ...it's just a shame you had to do it with your head."

Elli chuckled at her boss's grin. "Anything to help, boss."

IT TURNED out billionaires were fussbudgets. Or, at least, this one was. Aldo Costanza insisted on carrying Elli upstairs. She barely had time to deal with the flare of heat, this time all through her body, before he was unlocking her door and asking where her bedroom was. It was too surreal, being tucked into her bed by a handsome billionaire, all the while her head spinning.

She half expected him to take a seat beside her bed and sit some kind of guard as she slept, but instead, he apologized profusely, saying he had a meeting he couldn't rearrange, but that he would check up on her soon. After more passionate apologies, he finally left, but not before making sure she had water, aspirin, and a phone within arm's reach.

Once he was gone, Elli lay in bed for a long while, but couldn't sleep. The exhaustion was there, but it warred with her ever-active mind. Even a concussion couldn't stop Elli from overthinking things. She crawled out from under the covers that Aldo had fastidiously tucked around her, cranked up the heat, and made herself some tea—some kind of blend Vivienne said was good for relaxing. By the time the water boiled, her legs were wobbly and she was glad to curl up on the couch with her favorite blanket, listening to the wind outside her windows.

Her apartment was tiny, but she didn't care about that—the view from the windows over Venice's Lagoon made it worth the squeeze. Resting her aching head against a pillow, she saw the ice and fog covering the gondoliers, jostling together at their moorings, the usually crowded streets almost empty. It would be

Christmas soon, but if this weather held up, it would be a subdued event. Elli liked to walk the streets at night during the festive period—being alone in the world had never bothered her much. She would eat food from street vendors and soak in the atmosphere, thinking about her mother who had died when Elli was only eighteen. Her father had been long gone; Elli didn't even know who or where he was. And her older brother, Enzo, had died the year previously from the same cancer that took their mother.

Sadness touched Elli as Enzo filled her mind. Nearly a decade older, he had been her hero—companion, teacher, protector—or at least, he had taught her how to protect herself. He had been an architect, designing some of the most beautiful hotels in Italy with his best friend, Indio. The sadness that Enzo's memory always brought Elli was gently sidelined by a warm rush through her veins when she thought suddenly of Indio.

Indio Navaro had been her first crush—her first love. She closed her eyes now and thought of his dark curls, his swarthy caramel skin, and his bright green eyes. She remembered the first time she had seen him when she was just nine and he was eighteen. God, he had looked like an Adonis, so beautiful, with huge eyes, a perfectly symmetrical face, and a hard, toned body. No teenage acne or awkwardness for Indio, and even at her young age, Elli had known she would never again see such a beautiful man in her life. And he was beautiful—handsome wasn't strong enough word for Indio Navaro—not just physically perfect, but the kindest, sweetest, strongest man she had ever known. For his part, Indio had stayed true to the code—never fool around with your best friend's sister—but he had adored Elli too and would spend hours with her, even when Enzo wasn't there. They were the moon and the sun to each other.

But then, when Elli was twenty, a couple of years after her mother had died, something had happened between Enzo and Indio—something neither of them would ever talk about—and when Indio had come to say goodbye to Elli, her heart had been broken.

"Please don't go," she had begged him. "I love you so much, Indio. I always have."

Indio had looked shattered, and for a moment, she had thought he might kiss her. Instead, he had leaned his forehead against hers, and to her astonishment, she had felt tears on his cheeks. "Elli Bella, I ..." He had choked on the words and, not caring anymore about what was right, she had pressed her lips to his.

"Tell me you love me ...please, Indio, say it just once. I know you do. I know it in my soul ..."

Indio had grabbed her head and kissed her roughly, then pulled away, his hands dropping from her, his eyes closed. "I can't. I'm sorry, cara mia, I can't."

And then he was gone, and Elli had curled up into a little ball, her heart destroyed. When Enzo, pale and hollow-eyed came to find her, she hadn't attacked him or blamed him. He was her brother after all.

Indio didn't love me enough, Elli told herself for years, trying to mend her heart, but something had always told her that wasn't the truth. But when Enzo had died, her chance of finding out what had really happened between him and Indio was gone. Indio had left Venice and gone to Rome. Elli made herself stay away from searching for him on the internet or reading about him in magazines. She knew he was a big deal in Rome and abroad, his property nous and artistic aesthetic making him a billionaire. He had dated a string of beautiful women and married and divorced a former Miss World within a year, but lately, had disappeared—gone to ground.

Elli sighed and pushed the thoughts of Indio away. She was a master of that; it was just in quiet moments like this one that she wished he was here with her, watching old movies and cuddling under a blanket like back in the old days. In bed alone, sometimes Elli would think about what it might have been like to have sex with him, his big body covering her tiny one, his mouth on hers.

You are twenty-eight and still behaving like a lovesick teenager. Maybe it was the concussion that made her feel so melancholy. She dragged her thoughts back to Aldo Constanza and smiled. What a sweetheart of a man. His gaze had been intense on hers a couple of times, and her stomach had curled, warming at being so obviously admired.

Her phone beeped from the bedroom. Grumbling, Elli emerged from her cozy nook in the corner of the couch, carrying her blanket with her. She made her way the short distance to the bedroom and read the text message.

YOU MAY BE HURTING, girl, but you are also a magician. Aldo Constanza is investing—and he's investing BIG. I love you! Call me if you need anything! Viv xxx

ELLI SMILED and returned to the couch. Putting the phone on speaker so she could keep her hands curled around the mug before all the warmth of the tea dissipated, she dialed the office.

"Hey, bruiser!" Vivienne's voice was typically cheerful, but with an edge of worry. "I didn't wake you up, did I? How's the head?"

Elli grinned, although her head ached badly now. "Better hearing that news. No, I wasn't asleep."

"You should've been," lectured Vivienne. "You're supposed to be resting."

"You texted me," Elli reminded her. She took a sip of the tea and grimaced, wishing she could magically transport honey from the kitchen to the couch. "But trust me, Aldo tried to make sure I did."

"Aldo?" Vivienne repeated.

"He carried me in." Elli tried to gloss past that detail. "Oh, god, Viv, I'm so happy for y you—for the magazine. Thank god I didn't jinx it."

"Far from it, El ... don't think you're getting away without giving me all the dirt! But

Constanza had one little request. That you do an interview with him for the magazine—an in depth, not a puff piece, don't worry—when you're better. I think you have an admirer, Elli. A rich, handsome sweetheart of an admirer."

Elli flushed with pleasure. "He wants me to interview him?"

Vivienne sighed and laughed. "Trust you to focus on the work part—I'm telling you, that man wants to fu ..."

"Vivienne Marche, you are over-excited," Elli interrupted her, laughing and wincing at the corresponding twinge in her head. "Less than an hour ago, the guy was all but singing me a lullaby. Not exactly a precursor to a horizontal tango. Calm down."

"I'm just saying ...you need to get laid and there's nothing like a sex-god billionaire to get your rocks off."

Elli shook her head, grinning, although the thought wasn't exactly repulsive to her. Aching head or not, the shock of the accident had receded more than enough for her to fully realize that Aldo was gorgeous. "Viv, I'll talk to him to arrange the interview when I get back."

"Um ..." Vivienne suddenly sounded sheepish.

"What? What did you do?" Elli knew Vivienne's machinations of old, especially when it came to Elli's love life.

"Well, he kind of asked for your number, and I kind of gave it to him. I figured he rescued you, so ...was I wrong?"

Elli sighed. "No, it's fine. He probably won't call anyway."

Aldo Constanza did call that night, about eight p.m., while Elli was stubbornly trying to read in defiance of a headache that just wouldn't completely go away and contemplating what to eat for her supper, seeing as her fridge was empty.

"How are you feeling, Elliana?"

His voice was deep, sexy, and weirdly already familiar. She settled herself back against the pillows, smiling. Just because she hadn't thought he'd call didn't mean she hadn't hoped. "I'm okay. Just a little tired now. Thank you for today, Mr. Constanza. I mean it."

"Please call me Aldo. Despite the circumstances and you being hurt, it was entirely my pleasure. Have you talked to Vivienne at all?"

"I have, and she told me about your request. It would be my honor."

"Then it's settled. Perhaps we can talk about it when you've recovered, but I also wanted to ask if I may take you to dinner tonight?"

Elli blinked, glancing down at her ratty old pajamas, then catching a glimpse of her disastrous hair, which she'd only just revealed from beneath the bandage. "Tonight?"

Aldo gave a soft laugh. "Blame Vivienne—she was fretting about you not having any food in your home. I take it that's not unusual?"

Elli didn't know how to react to that. "Um, well, yes, that is true. Unless you consider breakfast cereal a meal."

"I do not," he chuckled. God, he had a sexy laugh. "But what am I thinking? You probably don't feel like going out in your condition and this weather. May I be so bold as to suggest I bring dinner to you?"

And for the life of her, Elli had no good reason to say no.

An hour later, after she had panicked after hanging up the phone, dashing around the place, tidying it and herself, and she didn't know why she had worried. He'd seen virtually everything already. Well ... not everything. A loud knock on the door interrupted that particular train of thought. She hurried over and opened the door, taking in the vision of the crazy hot billionaire standing behind a stack of two large, steaming-hot pizzas. "One vegetarian and one pepperoni," he greeted her. "I didn't know if you eat meat."

"Oh, so Viv didn't tell you everything?" Elli grinned at him, and he smiled somewhat sheepishly.

"Sorry." He eased the pizza boxes onto her little dinner table. "Have I railroaded you?"

She put her hand on his arm—hey, any excuse to touch the —guy. "Not at all. I'm just kidding. Can I take your coat?"

Already, she thought of him as a tailored suit guy, so when he slipped out of his long coat to reveal a dark navy sweater and jeans, the navy bringing out the hazel in his eyes, she was taken aback—and impressed. He caught her expression and smiled.

"You like my sweater?"

No, actually, it's you I like, she wanted to say. She breathed in his clean, woody scent and felt a pulse begin to beat between her legs. Aldo held her gaze, then smiled, stroking his hand on her cheek. God, his hands ...

"Whatever you are thinking, cara mia, I am thinking too. But

I am aware you have a pretty severe concussion, so maybe, tonight, we should just eat."

Elli flushed, then giggled, shaking her head. On some men, it might have been presumption. With Aldo, it came across as devastating candor. No games, apparently. She liked that. "I'm sorry, I'm all over the place. Please, have a seat."

They ate most of the two pizzas as they chatted, and Elli began to feel much more relaxed. Aldo was fun, intelligent, and god, he was sexy, his big frame dominating her small couch. His arm lay across the back of it, and she could feel the heat of his skin as his fingers lay inches from the back of her neck. He was easy to talk to as they discussed his business and his investment in the magazine. Elli was starting to feel excited about the forthcoming interview and told him so.

He smiled. "I'm glad ...but only when you are fully recovered, little one. Then, I hope, you will come to my home and we will do the interview there. Afterward, perhaps you would dine with me?"

Elli blushed with pleasure. "I would like that very much."

Just before ten p.m., he announced it was time he left so she could get some rest. He kissed her hand, his warm lips seeming to linger over her skin, while Elli stood in the doorway, heartrate surging. "I don't recall when I have spent such a pleasurable evening," he said.

She looked up at him, mesmerized by his eyes. "Me too. Thank you, Aldo. This day has been so much better than it deserved to be."

He touched a finger to her cheek and was gone.

That night, for the first time in eight years, it wasn't Indio who Elli dreamed of. And in the morning, a huge hamper of luxury food was waiting for her outside her door, with the note:

Just so you don't starve while you recover, cara mia. I look forward to our next meeting. Aldo.

In amongst the expensive gourmet food was a box of her favorite breakfast cereal.

A WEEK LATER, she was deemed by Vivienne to be fit enough to return to work, and two days later, she was being driven out to Aldo's villa in Mira. As she approached, she gave a small gasp. The villa was huge and utterly Italian, but Elli had learned enough from her brother and Indio to know what was old and what was new. This villa was a recent build, which didn't detract from its beauty one bit. Its features were simpatico with the Italian countryside around it, and although opulent, it shone with good taste.

Elli's heart was pounding even harder now. The design of it, the feel …it reminded her of the houses Indio and her brother had designed and built at the beginning of their partnership, albeit, on a much, much larger scale. This has to be one of Indio's, she thought, and she felt tears welling to the surface.

No. No, I will not ruin this by thinking about him, she thought to herself fiercely, and when the car pulled up and Aldo came out to meet her with a smile on his face, she pushed all thoughts of Indio to the back of her mind.

"Bella Elli, it has been too long," he said, kissing her cheek and lingering just a little too long. Elli felt her body respond, but she reminded herself to act professionally and smiled back at him.

"This is a stunning villa, Aldo."

Aldo beamed at her. "Thank you. I could give you the tour if you'd like."

"Shall we do the interview first? Get the work part out of the way?" Too late, she realized what that sounded like and blushed furiously. Aldo laughed.

"That sounds …promising."

Later, Elli would be able to narrow it down to three particular moments when she knew she would be sleeping with Aldo Constanza that night. The first was when they were talking about his work with starving children in Uganda, and he was talking with such passion and commitment that it touched Elli's heart. Here was a man unafraid to wear his heart on his sleeve.

The second was when, after a delicious and luxurious dinner, they took a walk around his grounds, and he took her hand, bringing the inside of her wrist to his lips and kissing it softly.

The third was when, a moment after that, he'd turned to her and taken her in his arms, smoothing the hair away from her face.

"Bella Elliana ...I'm going to kiss you now, then I'm going to take you to my bed, undress you, and kiss every part of your delicious body."

Elli gasped a little, feeling her sex dampen and quiver at his coarse but sexy-as-all-hell words. His lips met hers, and they kissed, all passion and no hesitation.

In a flash, they were in his bedroom and he was stripping her slowly, lingering over each piece of exposed skin until she was trembling with desire. He swept her onto the bed and knelt over her as he freed his cock from his jeans, stroking the length of it and enjoying her lust and admiration.

"All this is for you, Elli Bella."

Elli didn't have time to register what he'd called her before he thrust his cock deep inside her, hitching her legs around his waist and ramming his hips hard against hers. Elli's body acted as if she had no control over it, her back arching as he fucked her, her belly pressing against his, and her nipples so reacting so sensitively that when they brushed against his pecs, she screamed with pleasure.

Aldo was a masterful, dominant lover who enjoyed pinning

her to his bed, not letting her recover between orgasms, his face hard and focused as his cock thrust deeper and deeper inside of her.

"Mio Dio, you are a beautiful woman. Mio Dio ..."

They came together, Elli gasping and moaning as Aldo groaned, pumping thick, creamy come deep inside her belly. He kissed her tenderly as they panted for breath.

"Sweet Elli, you have made me so happy, so happy ..."

She smiled at him. "That was incredible, Aldo ...just as I dreamed it would be."

Aldo looked boyish as he grinned in delight. "You dreamed of me?"

"I did." Elli kissed his lips, his neck, then made her way down his body and took his cock in her mouth, teasing the long shaft with her tongue, feeling it quiver and harden under her touch. Aldo, on his back now, was stroking her hair.

"God, yes, Elli, that's so good, so good ..."

She brought him to near orgasm, then straddled him, impaling herself onto him with a soft moan. God, she wanted this man, his machismo, and his strength. She rode him hard, his hands squeezing and caressing her breasts, then stroking her belly, his thumb pressing deeply into the hollow of her navel.

As the intensity built, Aldo flipped her onto her back and began to thrust harder and harder, almost violent in his need for her. Elli clung to him, her fingernails digging into his shoulders. Aldo gripped her wrists and forced her hands onto the bed. This man likes being in control, Elli thought as another shattering orgasm ripped through her body. Aldo, almost frenzied now, bit down hard on her shoulder, and she yelped in surprise and pain as he came, shuddering and groaning, his seed shooting deep inside of her.

"Are you mine, Elli?"

She nodded, breathless, and Aldo took her clit into his

mouth and made her come over and over until she begged him to stop, exhausted and sated.

Aldo wasn't nearly done yet. He covered her body with his, kissing her mouth and smoothing the damp hair away from her face. "If you only knew how much I wanted you the moment I saw you on that street." He grinned and chuckled softly. "Even covered in blood, you were beautiful."

Elli frowned a little. Was she too sensitive? Because that sounded a little weird. Aldo saw her expression. "I just mean, you could be covered in dirt or blood or anything, and I would still think you were the most beautiful woman I'd ever seen. Forgive me. I realize now what I said might have sounded strange."

Elli relaxed, her arms around his neck. Aldo Constanza had just fucked her into next week and her body felt strangely soft, as if all her limbs and bones had been liquified. "You're forgiven. Aldo ...it's been the most incredible night."

He stroked a hand down the length of her. "You'll stay the night?"

She half-smiled. "I'm torn. Professionally speaking, I haven't been at all professional." They both laughed. "But the thought of leaving you naked in this bed to go home to my cold one ..."

He kissed her again, pushing her legs apart, his cock already hard again. "Then stay," he said, thrusting into her. "Stay and let's do this all night long ..."

ELLI WOKE A LITTLE BEFORE DAWN, her throat dry. Aldo lay on his stomach next to her, his big arm thrown across her. She studied him for a long moment, her new lover. His features were made to look tense, she decided, and smoothed the crease between his eyes that made him look angry. She smiled as it immediately settled back into a line, then gently removed Aldo's arm from around her waist. She slid from the bed, snagging his shirt and wrapping it around her body. She padded through the quiet villa, down to the large kitchen, and helped herself to a bottle of water from the vast, well-stocked refrigerator, grinning to herself at the difference between this one and her own. She even recognized some of the same foods Aldo had sent to her in the hamper. A man of good taste—of particular tastes. She went to the hallway and tried the doorway to one of the balconies. It opened, and she stepped out into the freezing cold night. The cold took her breath away, but it cooled her too-hot body. It had been a long time since she'd shared a bed with someone else, and it felt strange and a little claustrophobic.

She started slightly as Aldo slid his arms around her waist. "You'll catch your death out here," he murmured into her ear, and she grinned, moving to turn in his arms.

"No, stay like that," he said, and slipped his hand between her legs, parting them. Elli gasped as he thrust his cock into her from behind, his hand on her belly to keep her close as he fucked her. She rested her head back on his shoulder, panting for air. Her bare feet were freezing against the ice-cold stone of the balcony.

"Bend over the balcony for me, Principessa. Put your feet on mine if they are cold."

She did both, loving the adventure of it and feeling him grip her hips tightly as he thrust his cock deeper and deeper into her. The cold stone bit into her breasts as she gripped the balcony, but she didn't care. The sensations he sent through her body were exquisite. She heard him groan and felt him come, reveling in the feeling of his huge cock filling her. Aldo panted for air, then swept her up in his arms, carrying her inside. Just before they got to the bedroom, Elli saw a painting she hadn't noticed earlier. "Wait." She gazed up at it. The woman in the picture had an ethereal beauty—her dark brown hair was piled up on top of her head and her large brown eyes were soulful—but it was the sadness in them that took Elli's breath away. She had known this sadness, felt this utter desolation and heartbreak ...three times. "Who is she?"

Aldo's eyes were suddenly wary. "Her name was Yvetta. She was my lover a few years ago."

"What happened to her?"

Aldo looked away from her gaze. Elli touched his cheek lightly. "Aldo, I'm sorry. I didn't mean to pry—"

"It's all right." He coughed, clearing emotion from his throat and looking back at her with obvious grief on his face. "She died. No, that doesn't even cover it ...she was murdered. By an enemy of mine."

"Oh my god, Aldo!" Elli said in shock.

He nodded, putting her down and running a hand through his short hair. "He was obsessed with her and kept trying to steal her from me. When she wouldn't go to him, he killed her on what would have been our wedding day."

Elli gave a horrified gasp. She touched Aldo's face again, framing it with her hands. "God, Aldo ...I'm so sorry. I can't begin to imagine."

"I found her," he said bleakly, looking up at the painting, his voice breaking. "I found her dead, in her wedding dress, covered in blood. My beautiful Yvetta ..."

Elli wrapped her arms around him and comforted him as Aldo tried to regain his composure. They stood for a while, just embracing, before Elli led him back to bed. They made love slowly this time, tenderly, and when they were finally sated, Aldo laid his head on her chest and they slept.

THE NEXT DAY WAS A SATURDAY, thankfully, and when Elli opened her eyes it was already mid-morning. The bed beside her was empty, and at the end of the bed, a fresh robe was placed, a note attached.

Help yourself to anything you need, my sweet girl. I'll be down in my study when you are ready. A.

Elli smiled and went into the en-suite bathroom, which was as palatial as the rest of the rooms in this villa. Elli smiled to herself—Aldo Constanza did not do anything small ...his business, his house, his lovemaking ...

Stepping into the shower, Elli felt relief as the warm water cascaded over her body. Soaping herself, she saw souvenirs of the night before written on her body; the imprint of Aldo's teeth on her shoulder and bruises on her wrists and arms. There were bruises the shape of his fingertips on her hips. It didn't bother her; they were marks of passion and desire, not cruelty or violence.

She dressed quickly, stuffing her underwear into her purse, then went down to find Aldo.

He looked up as she came in and smiled. "Good morning, beautiful." He stood to greet her, brushing his lips tenderly against hers. "How did you sleep?"

"Wonderfully, thank you." She looked at his open lap-top. "I don't want to disturb you, though."

Aldo smiled. "It is unfortunate that I do have to work today. May I ask Umberto to drive you home?"

Elli smiled. "Of course. Thank you. And thank you for last night."

He kissed her again. "May I see you again, Elli?"

She smiled and nodded. "I would like that. But, Aldo, I do have to say ...I don't want this to interfere with my work. It is very important to me."

"I understand. I would never place any expectations on you, my sweet girl. Please, won't you stay and have brunch with me before you leave? I'll ask Umberto to bring the car around in an hour."

"If it won't keep you from your work," she said, but his hands were already snaking under her skirt and encountering bare skin. She grinned, looking up at him from beneath her lashes.

"I don't put yesterday's underwear on."

With a feral growl, Aldo pulled her into his arms and kissed her, his lips rough against hers. He fucked her against the wall of his study, and it was almost animalistic the way he took her, pinning her hands above her head and thrusting deep and long into her cunt.

AN HOUR LATER, she was being driven through the snow back to her apartment. Before she got there, feeling energized and joyful, she decided she would go grocery shopping and asked the car to change directions.

Wandering around the Christmas markets, she spent a leisurely afternoon shopping and didn't notice how late it had gotten until the streets were emptying. Elli hauled her full bags back toward her apartment, contemplating what she might make with the fresh ingredients.

It began with a prickle up her spine as she walked down a dark alleyway. Elli stopped and turned. Though an alleyway could suggest danger to some, this one was as familiar to Elli as any main road. She'd never felt any kind of fear while walking through it, regardless of the time of day. But now, she felt as if someone were watching her. She sucked in a breath and checked every dark corner she could see. Nothing. Not even a breeze. Picking up her pace, she walked quickly back to her apartment., Relocking the door behind her, she put her grocery bags down. Walking into her own home, she should've immediately felt secure, but the feeling persisted. Hesitating just a second, she grabbed a knife from the kitchen drawer.

Her apartment was only three rooms, but she checked everywhere she could think of. Nothing and no one. Elli shook her head. She had never been one to be paranoid, so why now? Was it just the seismic shift in her life from a week ago? A night ago?

"It must be that," she said aloud to herself, feeling her body finally relax, and went to unpack her groceries.

She had just finished cleaning up the kitchen and was getting into bed as her cell phone rang. "Hello, sweet girl. I just wanted to make sure that you're okay?"

Elli smiled. "I'm good, Aldo, thank you. I've had a very decadent afternoon and stocked my refrigerator."

Aldo laughed. "I'm glad to hear it, although I do wish I was with you. I realized tonight what a big, empty house this is."

Elli felt a little uncomfortable. "There'll be other nights, Aldo."

"Oh, I know, sweet girl. What are you doing now?"

"Just about to go to bed."

"Naked?" He sounded like a hopeful little boy, and she laughed.

"Of course."

"Hmm, now I'm beginning to visualize that, and it's very, very nice ..." His voice dropped low. "If I were with you, I'd be running my hands down your soft skin, cupping your beautiful breasts ...will you do that for me, cara mia, and pretend it's me touching you?"

Elli closed her eyes and did as he asked, enjoying the sensuality of his voice purring down the phone. She stroked her hand down her body, over her breasts. "What else would do you do to me?"

"I would circle your bellybutton with my thumb, gently, over and over until I could feel your belly quiver under my touch."

Elli moaned softly, turned on by his words and the feel of her hand on her belly. "Then lower, my love, down into your sex, your delicious tight little cunt. I would caress your clit until it was hard and so sensitive that you wanted to scream. Spread your legs wide, my baby, and stroke yourself for me."

Elli gasped as she obeyed him. "Aldo ...Aldo ...are you touching yourself?"

He gave a low, amused chuckle. "You better believe it, sweetheart. Now, I want you to imagine my cock is sliding into you, so slowly that you get annoyed with me and scream at me to fuck you ..."

"Wait," Elli gasped, panting. She reached over to her nightstand and grabbed her vibrator. She pushed it inside of herself, moaning as she imagined it was his cock.

"Good. That's good, sweet girl. My cock is inside you now, filling you, plowing deep inside you again and again until you see stars in your eyes ...Elli?"

Almost delirious, Elli gasped her "Yes?"

"Are you free tomorrow? Can I come see you?"

Elli came as she sighed, "Yes, yes, yes ..."

Aldo gave a satisfied laugh. "Good ...tomorrow, then?"

Elli chuckled, still catching her breath. "Tomorrow, Aldo."

All traces of her earlier fear had long fled as she said goodnight and fell straight asleep, thoroughly sated.

Two weeks later—two long weeks full of every manner of fucking, whether or not Elli and Aldo were in the same —room— Vivienne met with Elli for lunch. After an enjoyable thirty minutes spent discussing everything under the sun, Vivienne finally got around to work talk. Only, because Vivienne was Vivienne and her radar missed nothing, work had a double meaning. "Girl, this article is one of your best. Hands down. How'd you get him to open up so much?"

Elli could feel her face burn a little, thinking of all the different kinds of opening up she and Aldo had been doing. "He's very ... loquacious when you get him on the right topic. His work in Uganda, his love of art. He even told me some stuff about his personal life, but I felt it didn't add anything to the article and it would be taking advantage of a personal tragedy."

. "You're sleeping with him," Vivienne said bluntly, not asking.

Hiding things from her best friend was an impossibility. "Maybe ..."

Vivienne grinned from ear to ear. "Well, hallelujah. So, are you two an 'item?'"

Elli laughed then, taking a sip of wine. "Yeah, Grandma, we're a-courtin'. No, I think, for me, it's just a pleasant fling."

"And what about for him?" Vivienne pressed, pushing her plate back and waving a waiter over to remove it before refilling her glass. "Aldo Constanza doesn't strike me as a man to do things by half. You sure he doesn't think you two are serious?"

Elli shrugged. "We haven't talked about it, but, Viv, I won't let it affect my work here, I swear. I'm scared that if I get too involved and it ends badly, it could mean Aldo withdrawing his investment."

Vivienne looked vaguely horrified. "Elli, your sex life is your business. Don't let Aldo dictate things like that."

"Oh, he's not, Viv. I'm sorry if it came out that way. I mean, my work is my passion. That's the most important thing to me."

Studying her intently, Vivienne covered Elli's hand with her own. "Would you say that if we were talking about Indio Navaro?"

A bolt of pain shot through Elli, leaving her feeling like she'd been ambushed. "But we're not."

Immediately remorseful, Vivienne rounded the table and sat down beside Ellie, hugging her close. "Oh, sweetheart. I say this is as your friend and because I love you. It's been eight years, Elli. You have to start looking to the future. Indio's not coming back, however much you keep your heart hidden from everyone else. Aldo Constanza is gorgeous, delicious, and he believes in your work."

Elli sat back, looking away for a second to regain her composure. "I know, and you're right about ...Indio." Why did it still hurt so much to say his name? It was like a thousand swords being plunged into her heart. Elli rubbed her eyes and Vivienne smiled.

"If I did that, I'd look like a panda," she said. "I will never stop being jealous of the fact you don't have to wear makeup, girl. Just don't throw this thing with Aldo away because of an old attachment, no matter how much Indio once meant to you. That's all I'm saying."

"He didn't once mean something to me," Elli muttered, reaching for her empty wine glass just to do something with her hands. "He still does, Viv."

"And he always will, I know. But you can temper that meaning so that you still have a chance at a meaningful relationship, Elliana. A real relationship."

"As opposed to a ghost one." Elli nodded, stifling a sigh. "Yes. Yes. I know."

ALDO CAME to meet her as Elli was leaving the office. He kissed her passionately, not caring who saw them on the crowded street.

"Mm, I've missed you today, Elli Bella."

Elli hated that he called her that—it had been Indio's nickname for her. Then she pulled herself up—so what? It was as sweet a name for her and Indio didn't own it. He would never say those words again, so what did it matter? She smiled up at Aldo, stroking the short hair over his ear.

"Shall we spend tonight at my place? We always seem to be going to your home."

Aldo tightened his arms around her. "Ah, but there's more space at mine. Come back with me, Elli. I have a surprise for you."

Elli pushed away from the annoyance she felt. Every time she had seen Aldo since that first time when they had eaten pizza together, it had been assumed that they would spend the night at his villa. Did he think her place wasn't suitable for a man such as himself? She didn't want to argue, though, not out in public like this, so she agreed, giving him a half-smile as he took her hand and led her to his car.

At his villa, he placed his hands over her eyes and then steered her into his vast living room. "Open."

Elli opened her eyes and gave a delighted laugh. A huge Christmas tree stood, its lights twinkling in the dim light of the living room. "Oh, Aldo, it's so beautiful."

He kissed the soft skin on the inside of her wrist. "I remember you telling me that you missed having Christmas with your family and that your apartment was too small for you to have a tree. So I thought of this."

Elli felt tears in her eyes and felt badly for her earlier irritation. She touched Aldo's face, then went to examine the tree. She breathed in the fresh scent of pine and admired the glitter and sparkle of the gold decorations. It was opulent, extravagant, and exquisitely decorated—a far cry from when Enzo and Indio used to haul in a bedraggled tree from the garden and make paper decorations for it. Elli knew that it was improbable that Aldo had decorated this tree himself, but it was still a thoughtful gesture.

She felt his hand on her back. "You like it?"

She nodded, turning to kiss him. "It's beautiful."

He took her face in his hands, studying her eyes. "It pales in comparison to you, beautiful girl." His lips touched hers and Elli sank into the kiss, Aldo's hands roaming over her body leisurely before his fingers pulled at the zipper of her dress. She grinned at him as the dress fell to the floor, and Aldo smiled back, pulling her to him roughly, so her belly curved against his shirt. "There is no comparison when I see your body like this, except for when ..." And he unclasped her bra and drew her panties down. "You should always be naked, Elliana Moretti. The world would thank you. I have a gift for you."

He bent down and picked up a box, giftwrapped in silver and gold with an off-white bow. Carefully, Elli peeled the paper away, wanting to save it for no reason other than the memory. The box beneath matched the wrapping paper, metallic colors gleaming in the low light as Elli slid her thumbs into an indentation on each end and popped the lid off. She drew in her breath at the incredible necklace embedded in soft velvet, white gold and diamonds glistening at her like the gleam in Aldo's eyes when she looked up to thank him

"It's beautiful," she murmured, lifting it out and starting to put it to her neck, then stopping in confusion as she realized that there was a lot more to the opulent strand than she had initially thought.

Smiling, Aldo reached for the piece of jewelry. "It's a body chain. Here let me put it on for you."

He put the delicate chain over her head, the light metal feeling cool across her bare skin, and crisscrossed it between her breasts, over her belly, and between her legs. Elli looked down at herself in amazement; she had to admit it looked good against her caramel skin, the diamonds twinkling in the light of the Christmas tree's own illuminations.

Aldo stepped back and admired her body. "Wow. Just wow ... Elli, you have the body of a goddess ..."

Elli smiled, feeling very sensual now and completely sexy in this man's presence. Aldo quietly swept her off of her feet and lay her on the thick carpet before stripping off his tie. "I'm going to touch you now, Elli, and caress you until you beg for my cock ...but I want to make you shiver in anticipation and the best way to do that is ..." He wound his tie around her eyes, blindfolding her. Elli shivered straight away, feeling vulnerable, and she heard Aldo give a low chuckle. "That's right, Elliana ...you're at my mercy."

Her breath hitching and trembling, she waited for his touch.


ALDO GAZED down at the beautiful woman on his carpet and smiled. This is what he had wanted--having her helpless, desperate for his touch. He began by kissing her lips and throat, then trailing his lips across her collar bones, taking each nipple into his mouth and teasing the small bud of each, stroking his hand down her soft belly and between her legs, then stopping just before he reached her clit, teasing and tormenting her. He stripped off his clothes, hefting the weight of his cock in his hand as it hardened at the sight of her. He lay down, taking her hands and pinning them above her head, his body covering hers, his weight on her tiny frame.

"You are mine tonight, Elliana."

Elli gasped as he began to push his cock into her, then withdrew, doing it again and again until she nearly screamed with frustration, then thrust it in deep, pushing her legs apart until he knew her hips were objecting, sore and burning. Good. In the morning, he wanted her to ache and to feel the aftermath of the way he was going to fuck her tonight. Feel it in every part of her delicious body. As his thrusts began to get hard and deeper, he gathered her to him, his mouth on her lips, her throat, his teeth biting her shoulders, her breasts. Elli clung to him as his lovemaking became almost frenzied and he heard her give a small cry of pain as he rammed his cock deeper inside her, but he ignored it. She was his and his alone.

He came, shuddering and groaning her name as she panted beneath him. He kissed her tenderly, stroking her clit until she too came. He rolled off her and propped himself up on his elbow to watch her as she caught her breath. He pushed the blindfold from her eyes and studied them. "Principessa, was that not good for you?"

Elli nodded, but he could see wariness and hesitation in her eyes. "It was, Aldo ...thank you."

He laughed. "You're thanking me for sex?"

Elli chuckled too, running her hand over her face. "Sorry, I'm just a little dazed."

"Do you feel well?"

"Oh, yes, fine. Just a little ...I've never had sex like that before and it ...scared me a little. The intensity. Being blindfolded." She chewed her bottom lip nervously as she looked up at him.

Aldo frowned. "You're not scared of me, surely?" He leaned in and kissed her lips softly. "You need never be afraid of me, sweet one."

But Elli didn't look convinced, and Aldo decided that he needed to be tender from now on. "I'm sorry if I frightened you, Elli. I had not thought that it might be too much, but now I can see it was. Please don't be scared."

She relaxed a little, half-smiling at him. "I'm just not as experienced as some women you might have dated. I'm a solitary creature by nature, Aldo. I have never felt the need to be coupled-up, or to always be in a relationship. The men I have slept with have always been good friends first. With you, it's different."

"We're not friends?" He felt a little stung and Elli touched his face.

"Of course we are, Aldo. I meant those other men were friends of long-standing, who just happened, at different moments, to be the right guy at the right time. You and I, we had an unusual start."

Aldo smiled at her, brushing his lips against hers. "Ours was romantic."

"Yeah," Elli looked at him askance, then laughed, "Concussions are so sexy."

He grinned. "You know what I mean."

She relented. "I do."

Reaching for another box, this one not wrapped, Aldo pressed it into Elli's hands. "This gift is more practical," he whispered in her ear, nibbling at it as she mildly protested what she deemed his 'extravagance,' then laughing when the box was open, revealing a simple white satin robe.

"I thought you liked me to wander around naked," she teased, kissing him in thanks.

"I do," he assured her, running his hands over her bare body once more. "But occasionally you might get chilly. I wouldn't want that ..."

He made sure, for the next hour or so, that she was anything but.

LATER, after they had dinner, they sat together, drinking scotch and watching the tree lights twinkle. Aldo stroked Elli's face and was quiet for a while. "Elli, spend Christmas with me. I hate to think of you alone in that tiny apartment. Spend it with me here, and we will eat too much food, drink too much champagne, and watch cheesy movies."

Elli half-smiled at him. "Are you sure? What about your family?"

Aldo sighed. "My father will be skiing with his wife in Austria; my younger brother, Antonio, is at college in the United States and does not intend to beg around his boring older brother. So, you see, I'm as alone as you."

He looked playfully mournful, but Elli felt stung by his words. Was she really that pathetic? She rubbed her forehead, trying to stave off a headache. She occasionally still got one in the aftermath of the concussion, but this one felt different.

"Are you all right?"

Always watching. The thought hit Elli, but she brushed it away. Don't be unfair, girl. He's just concerned. "A headache. Maybe I should go home."

He kissed her cheek and looked at her in concern. "Nonsense. Look, I'll get some aspirin for you, and some water, and you can go lie down."

When she was alone, Elli stared at the fire that Aldo had lit earlier, her emotions in turmoil. Was she just freaking out because it looked like she was about to embark on a relationship, whether she liked it or not—and she'd always studious avoided any type of commitment?

Vivienne's words came back to her. *Indio is gone, has been gone, for eight years. He's not coming back.*

"I know, I know," Elli murmured to herself and scrubbed at her face with her hands. She wasn't being fair to the lovely man in whose house she sat and in whose bed she experienced great sex and tenderness. Earlier, she had wanted to run when he got too intense, but she had talked herself down from it. It hadn't been violent or degrading, just more forceful than she was comfortable with. *Maybe that's what it feels like when it's not a fuck of convenience*, she told herself. *Because how would you know otherwise, Moretti?*

She squeezed her eyes shut, willing the headache to go away. A moment later, she felt a cold, damp towel being pressed against her forehead. It felt so good, she had to smile. "You are the sweetest man," she said softly, and Aldo responded by kissing her softly on her lips.

"Here, sweet girl, take these." He dropped a couple of aspirin in her hand and gave her the glass of water. "You should go lie down."

Elli opened her eyes and smiled at him. "If you come with me."

Aldo smoothed her hair. "Always."

They lay in bed, talking quietly, Aldo's hand stroking her face until she felt herself drifting off to sleep, her head still pounding.

The nightmare began as sweet memories of her and Indio and Enzo, down at Indio's mother's farmhouse in Tuscany, the summer heat, and picking olives in the grove. Indio teasing her, chasing her with a spider in his hand down the hill until they were both breathless, laughing and collapsing together. Indio plucking a bloom from the field of wild flowers and winding it around her finger. His lips were soft against hers. "Sposami?" Marry me?

Elli found herself in a white dress before she could even say yes, drifting down the hallway of Aldo Constanza's home. She was confused now ...why was she here, of all places? Was it still Indio she was marrying?

She pushed open the two huge, white doors in front of her to see an altar and Indio waiting for her at the end of the aisle. As she moved toward him, she saw her brother, her Enzo, step in front of her. "Don't do this, Elli, please. He's not who you think he is ...he's dangerous."

"I love him, Enzo. I've always loved him."

Her brother's image faded away, and she turned, smiling at

her groom.

"Listen to your brother." Another voice behind her. She turned. Yvetta, herself in a wedding dress, but with the hilt of a knife protruding from a huge blood stain on the bodice. Yvetta smiled, as beautiful as in Aldo's painting.

"He did this to me, Elli. He will do it to you too."

Elli shook her head. "You don't know him like I do ...he isn't capable."

Yvetta disappeared, and she was left alone with Indio. He took her hands and led her up the stairs toward a faceless priest who began to read the marriage ceremony.

"If any person should have an objection ..."

"Yes." A man's voice, broken and full of grief. Elli turned to see Aldo staggering up to the altar, heartbroken, his face streaming with tears.

"Please, Elli ...don't marry him ...he'll destroy you like you've destroyed me. Please ..."

Elli closed her eyes. "I'm sorry. I did love you for a time. I did."

When she opened, Aldo was gone and she was married. Her new husband looked down at her. "Come with me, my beautiful Elli."

Elli followed Indio into the hallway. In a flash, Indio cuffed her around the head, hard. Elli went down, confused and shocked. She looked around and the blood froze in her veins.

The knife Indio was holding was huge, lethal.

Oh, god, no ...

"I'm sorry, Elli, my beautiful Elli, but you know it has to end this way, don't you?" He walked slowly toward her, and she started to crawl backward.

He smiled down at her, his eyes soft. "I asked Aldo to come here, to see if you would be tempted, to see if you were true to me," he said. "I had to get him here, so that you could be tested, my darling. And you failed. You fell in love with Aldo Constanza and let him put his hands on you." He crouched next to her and grabbed her wrists, winding a rope around them. "He will find you here, stabbed to death. It will destroy him, and that's all I want. Well, apart from seeing you die and your beautiful skin split under my knife. I'm going to butcher you, my darling, put my knife into your belly over and over until you are dead. Right now, Elli ..."

Elli kicked out and caught him hard on the knee. Indio went down, howling, and Elli flipped over and started to pull herself away from him. She couldn't believe this. Indio, her beloved Indio, a killer.

It wasn't enough. Indio recovered and plunged the knife into the small of Elli's back. Elli cried out in agony, and laughing, Indio stabbed her again, an inch away from the first wound. Elli gasped for air as Indio flipped her onto her back and ripped open her dress. Elli's back arched as he drove the knife into her, pain ripping through her as he stabbed her again and again. Elli was losing consciousness from the pain.

"Stop," she whispered, weakening. "Stop. I'm dead ..."

But Indio's bloodlust wasn't sated. He stabbed her again, smiling as she moaned in agony.

Hot, sticky blood pumped out of her belly. Indio leaned over and kissed her mouth. "This is even better than marrying you might have been. Enzo knew the truth. Why do you think he warned me away from you all those years ago? Yvetta—poor, sweet Yvetta, loving me while knowing I could never love anyone but my Elli—still believing it when I put this very knife into her. You might call poor Yvetta a practice run."

No. No, she couldn't believe this. She wouldn't believe her Indio was a killer—and yet ...it had always lingered in his beautiful eyes. The violence. Had she mistaken it for passion?

"Why?" she whispered with the last of her strength as the last of her blood left her body. "I love you, only you, Indio."

Indio smiled. "And you always will, for eternity, my love …" And he slid the blade between her ribs, into her heart …

"No!" Elli screamed, bolting up in bed, then scrambling across the dark room. She tripped on something or other and went sprawling, nearly striking her head against a wall before she caught herself. Drenched in cold sweat, she trembled as she watched a figure rise in the bed a few feet away, broad shoulders turning toward her.

"Elliana?"

She relaxed slightly at Aldo's familiar voice, but not completely. Tension still sang through her, making every muscle ache.

"Elli?" he said again, getting out of bed and approaching her. Immediately, she stiffened against the wall, feeling the knife in her body and smelling her own blood.

"Elli," he murmured, stopping a few feet away and crouching. "Cara mia, what is it?"

The tenderness in his voice drained some of the terror from her veins. She moved hesitantly toward Aldo and he closed the narrow gap between them, his face wracked with shock and concern as he put his big, strong arms around her, not to hurt her, but to comfort and love.

"Sweet girl, what is it? You're safe here, you're safe …please, calm down, Elli."

She rode out the panic attack, breathing deeply and resting against his solid body. His lips were on her forehead as he stroked her back, whispering soft reassurances. "I'm sorry," she managed eventually. "It was a nightmare. God. Horrible, and stupid, and not real." Thankfully, he didn't press her for details.

She was sweating, but shivering violently. Aldo swept his hand onto her forehead. "Jesus, you're burning up."

He lifted Elli back into bed, and she was glad of it because she really was starting to feel sick, the nightmare receding in the face of real pain.

Aldo leaned down to kiss her gently and drew back at the expression of agony on her face. "I'm calling a doctor," he said firmly, and Elli didn't have the strength to protest.

ALDO'S BILLIONS commanded the highest level of service. The doctor arrived within the hour and wasted no time examining Elli and prescribing much-needed pain relief. While she rested, waiting for the pills to take effect, he spoke to Aldo just outside the room. Shortly, Aldo returned, sat on the edge of the bed, and held her hand. "Better, darling?"

"Much." Her eyes followed his lips as he pressed them to the inside of her wrist. "The doctor gave me the good stuff. What did he say?"

"Post-concussion syndrome," Aldo told her. "It should resolve itself in a few months, but he wants to do a CT, just to make sure nothing more insidious is going on."

"Can this really happen from a fall?" she asked. "I didn't think it was that bad ..."

He laughed humorlessly. "Elli, I'm the one who picked you up after that fall. You bled all over me on the way to the hospital. It was bad, sweet girl. Trust me. I'll set up an appointment for the scan in the next couple of days. And don't give me that look. I'm not dictating, love. I'm taking care of you."

Elli wrapped her fingers around his big hand. "I know. I know. But I've already missed enough work—"

"I called Vivienne—" he held up a hand, forestalling her immediate protest. "I knew she'd want to know, even if you might not have told her. She said to tell you that there are only a few days before you're off for the Christmas break anyway. You should take the time off and call her to let her know you're improving."

"Post-concussion syndrome," Elli muttered, shaking her head and immediately regretting it. He was just trying to help. She knew that. Why was she reacting so moodily? She reached for her iPad and batted Aldo's hands away as she started to do some fast research. After a few minutes of scanning different pages, she sighed and put the iPad aside. "This explains a lot."

"What does?"

"The symptoms list anxiety and irritability. If you knew me better, Aldo, you'd know that I'm pretty easy-going, but lately, I've felt on edge."

He smiled gently. "I know you better than you think, Elliana. And I had noticed, sweet girl."

She squeezed his hand guiltily. "I'm sorry, Aldo. I never meant to make you feel badly."

"Not at all …it's just, Elli, I'm in very great danger of falling in love with you," he confessed. "And somehow, it has seemed that you hold part of yourself back from me. I never want to make you feel obligated—so all I ask is that you're honest with me about how you feel."

Elli nodded, and for a few moments, she was silent. Finally, she decided it was time to confess. He'd been nothing but good to her and holding secrets back from him felt increasingly wrong. "Aldo, for a long time now, I've been stuck in a rut. I loved someone deeply. Entirely. It's been eight years, and he still haunts my dreams—and now my nightmares. He broke my heart, Aldo. Shattered it."

If she'd been afraid Aldo might react jealously—and she realized belatedly that she'd been somewhat worried about that, though he'd never shown a single jealous tendency yet—he calmed those fears immediately by sitting quietly and calmly, letting her speak, his expression betraying nothing but compassion.

"He was the moon and the sun to me," Elli went on, choking up a little. She was grateful for the reassuring pressure from Aldo's fingers on her hand, guiding her through the memories. "It's been eight years and I don't want to feel that way anymore." She reached up and touched his cheek. "That's as honest as I can be at this moment, Aldo. I love being with you, as a friend and as a lover. You are the first person since him who has broken down even some of my defenses. I can't promise I'll get there quickly, but I can promise to try. I do have feelings for you. I really do."

"As I do for you. Thank you for being so honest, Elli." Aldo bent his head and kissed her. Then he pulled off his clothes and slid into bed with her.

"Just to cuddle, don't worry," he said, as she settled comfortably into his arms. "I'll buy that you do actually have a headache."

Elli chuckled. "Which is getting better, by the way."

"Oh, really?"

"Really." She tilted her head back so he could kiss her. Aldo smoothed her hair back from her face, studying her.

"Still, I think you better get some sleep, baby. We have plenty of time." He told her what Vivienne had said. "So I'm going to ask again, but I won't be offended if you say no. Spend Christmas and New Years with me. I promise, as soon as you're feeling one hundred percent well, we will have a riot together. There are a few parties I've been invited to, which I would love for you to attend as my partner, if that suits you. And if not, we have the world at our fingertips, Elli. Anything, anywhere."

Elli smiled at him. "As long as I'm with you, I don't care what we do."

Her heart warmed when she saw the delight in his eyes. He is lovely, Elli thought now. Why the hell am I holding onto the ghost of what might have been, when this man is offering me the world?

Elli fell asleep locked in his arms, feeling something had shifted in her soul. Yes, she would try to be the woman Aldo thought she was, for him and for herself. Vivienne had been right.

It was time.

It was Christmas night and Elli and Aldo had finally stopped eating, lying with full bellies on his couch. Elli was groaning. "I seriously haven't eaten that much in years," she laughed and moaned as Aldo patted her bare stomach. "Don't. I'll explode."

"Sexy," Aldo said and laughed as she looked at him askance. "Elli, I'd like to thank you."

Elli looked at him in amazement. "You thank me? Aldo, look at this place. Look at what you've given me." She held up her wrist with the elegant and delicate diamond bracelet he had given her that morning, along with a host of other gifts. "You have given me something I thought lost to me. A family Christmas."

Aldo looked delighted, but he also shook his head. "You don't understand—Christmas for me, for the last few years, has been ...painful. Dark. You see, Yvetta was born on Christmas Day."

"Oh, Aldo, I'm sorry."

"No, you see? You have brought the light back into my life and into the holidays. You, Elli, have given me more than I ever thought possible. Oh, I've dated a few women since Yvetta died, but none could come close to you, my love." He leaned over and kissed her. "Elli, I told you a few days ago I was in danger of falling in love with you. These last few days have made me realize ...I'm no longer in danger. I am in love with you."

Ellis eyes filled with tears and she looked away. Aldo turned her face back to him. "Hey, hey. I don't expect or want you to feel the same until you do. There's no pressure, but I had to tell you that. I love you, Elliana Moretti."

Hot tears flooded down her cheeks as she kissed him. "Aldo ...I am changing. I can feel it, and you're the reason. I'm not there yet, but I'm starting to believe I will be. When I tell you I love you, I want it to be the absolute truth. But it's only you, now, Aldo. Only you."

It was only a partial lie, but Aldo seemed satisfied, grinning as he kissed her. "If only we hadn't been so gluttonous, I would take you on this couch right now."

She grinned. "Remember the time I was out on the balcony? I wouldn't mind reliving that, Mr. Constanza."

Aldo laughed. "Kinky girl. Just how kinky do you get, Ms. Moretti?"

She wrapped her arms around his neck. "What did you have in mind?"

"Hmm, how would you feel about restraints?"

Elli nodded slowly. "We could do that."

"Or perhaps we should invite someone to join us."

Elli's eyes opened wider. "A threesome?"

"What do you think? If we're getting real here, one of my fantasies is to watch you getting fucked by another man—as long as I could join in afterward, of course."

Elli thought about it for a long moment. "If it would turn you on, I wouldn't be against it. Who did you have in mind?"

Aldo adjusted himself so he could study her reaction. "A professional. Someone who can be trusted to be discreet."

"We're really talking about this, huh?" Elli was getting turned on now.

Aldo shifted, so he was on his knees, between her legs. He started to unbutton her jeans as he talked. "A young man. I'd ask him to undress you slowly so I could film your delectable body as he revealed each piece of skin." He tugged her jeans off and then pulled her t-shirt over her head. Elli grinned at him as he reached behind her to unclasp her bra, then took her nipple in his mouth greedily, sucking and teasing. His fingers were on her belly, stroking a circle around her deep navel. He smiled up at her as he released her nipple and moved to the other. "I would tell him to suck on your nipples as he finger-fucked your belly-button. Meanwhile, I would fuck your perfect ass, fingering your clit until you were begging for your sweet cunt to be filled."

He was sliding her panties down and then his mouth was on her clit, sucking and biting gently as Elli shivered and moaned. He paused for breath and smiled up at her. "Then I would ask him to fuck you, hard and rough, as I film his cock plunging in and out of your vagina." He slid two fingers into her damp cunt, then, and Elli writhed with pleasure.

"Yes, yes, Aldo ..."

A third finger slid inside her and she bucked against his hand. "Aldo, please, I want your cock. I need your cock inside me."

Aldo unzipped his pants and pulled his tumescent cock out, hard and quivering with arousal. "You want this, pretty girl?"

She nodded, and removing his hand, he obliged, fucking her hard as they began to describe kinkier ways to fuck. Aldo pinned her hands above her head as he tumbled her off the couch, onto the carpet. "I would love to see this incredible body in a leather harness," he said, clamping her legs around him and thrusting deep inside her. "There's just something about seeing you bound and helpless ...you weren't happy with the blindfold, but what if you could see what I was about to do to you, but you were still helpless to stop it? We could role play ...you could be the political prisoner. I could be your torturer ...I mean in a way you enjoyed," he added, seeing her eyes widen in surprise. "Nothing dangerous."

Elli relaxed, and they made love until they were both breathless and sated.

THEY GOT to live out one fantasy a few nights later. Aldo brought Elli to a New Year's Eve gala benefit held in one of the city's beautiful art museums. He introduced Elli to the man who had organized the gala, Maceo Bartoli, Venice's most celebrated art dealer. Elli liked the man immediately; his merry eyes and sweet smile belied the handsome face. With a pang, she realized mid-conversation that he reminded her so much of Indio that her chest began to hurt. Indio before the darkness, before he had left her. Maceo, his dark curls highlighted with silver, introduced Elli to his wife, Orianthi, a dark-haired beauty who had as much mischief in her eyes as her husband.

Ori bore Elli off to grab some drinks from the waiters who glided gracefully and discreetly around the gathering. Ori took an orange juice for herself, nodding down to her swollen belly. "This one won't let me drink for another three months."

She glows, Elli thought, warming to the other woman. "Is it your first?"

Ori shook her head, grabbing a canape from a tray and shoving it into her mouth in a way that Elli approved of. "No, we have a son too. Dario. He'll be eight soon—a charmer just like his dad. How long have you and Aldo been together?"

"Just a couple of months. It's early days. Have you known him long?"

"A while, but not well. He's kind of private. We don't see him out much. He's a home boy, I think, especially since his fiancée died. Awful, that was. I know something about being stabbed, so when Maceo met him, just after Yvetta died, Maceo told him about our history. I think it helped to talk to someone who knew what it was like."

"Maceo was stabbed?"

Ori shook her head. "No, I was. By a psychotic asshole who thought woman were possessions. But I nearly died, and Maceo went through hell. At least I had morphine. So he could relate to how Aldo felt. I hope it helped Aldo come to terms." She smiled at Elli. "Sorry, this is morbid. Let's change the subject. Are you in love with Aldo's home? I have such envy—not that Maceo wouldn't build one for me if I asked, but still. Whoever designed and built it for Aldo was a genius."

Elli felt her chest clench a little, but she asked the question anyway, keeping her tone casual. "Do you know who the architect was?"

Ori shook her head and leaned in conspiratorially. "I don't, but I heard he was some kind of player. Don't quote me on this, because I don't know for sure, but there were rumors that Yvetta was sleeping with him and that he may have had something to do with her murder. Of course, it was never proved and her murder is unsolved still. Hey, are you okay?"

Elli had paled. It couldn't be Indio. It couldn't. He would never hurt another person ...would he? Her nightmare came back to her and she shivered. She tried to smile at Ori. "I'm fine, honestly. Just such a lot of pain to cope with ...I just feel for Aldo."

"I know. Hey," Ori said, apparently wanting to distract her, "You're a journalist, right? I read your interview with Aldo and was inspired to read some of your other stuff. You're really talented."

Elli flushed with pleasure. It meant a lot to her that this lovely woman liked her work. "Thank you, Ori. You're very kind. If you ever wanted to tell your story, please think of me."

Ori hooted a little. "I'm not that interesting, believe me. Come on, let's look around."

AN HOUR LATER, Aldo, catching up with her, bent his mouth to her ear. "Meet me upstairs in the small balcony above the O' Keefe. Do you see it?"

She nodded and he disappeared. In a minute or so, she left Ori with Maceo and followed Aldo upstairs. The marbled hallway echoed with the chatter from below, but it was empty. As she got to the balcony, Aldo pulled her roughly into the little alcove that overlooked the gathering.

He kissed her passionately, then began to hitch up the skirt of her dress. Elli grinned, and when he encountered bare flesh instead of underwear, he looked up in surprise. "I thought something like this might happen ...well, I hoped it would," she whispered. Aldo stood and kissed her again.

"I'm going to fuck you first," he said. "Then we'll try something different."

He unzipped his pants and thrust deep inside her. Elli gasped, and Aldo clamped his hand over her mouth to silence her. It was a hard, quick, thrilling fuck, and they both came quickly.

Elli rammed her legs together as she felt his cum trailing down her leg, but it was such a turn on to play like this, the fear of being caught adding to the fun. Aldo lowered her skirt and turned her to face out of the balcony.

"Now," he said quietly, moving behind her. "The game is this. I'm going to fuck you from behind, but you must remain as if a statue, so that no one guesses what we are doing. Every time you feel my cock thrust into you, I want you to find a man in the gathering below, gaze at him, and pretend it's his cock fucking you. Control your orgasm. Concentrate on feeling it entirely in your cunt."

Elli felt him push up the back of her skirt and part her legs with his hand, caressing her clit from behind. She put her hands flat on the waist-height balcony balustrade to steady herself as Aldo entered her.

"Look at him, or him, or him ..." Aldo's murmur was low and masterful. "All of these men in this room would kill to fuck you, Elliana. Look at them."

As he fucked her, Elli obeyed his instructions and imagined that some of the good-looking, successful men in the gallery were the ones whose cocks was reaming her so hard. The international property magnate with the red-gold hair, or the sleek, blonde racehorse owner ...or Maceo Bartoli ...

Elli felt disloyal to Ori, looking at her husband with those thoughts, but Maceo was easily the handsomest man in the room. Aldo thrust harder as he neared his peak and keeping still was getting harder for Elli. She concentrated on Maceo, registering again how much he looked like Indio, and as she neared her peak, she felt Aldo's hand on her belly, pulling her back into the shadows. He muffled her cry with his mouth. They panted, calming themselves. They tidied up their clothes, grinning at each other.

"That was such a rush," she whispered, and Aldo grinned, nodding and kissing her again.

"Thank you for helping to fulfill that particular fantasy," he said, and she laughed.

"It was my pleasure."

The countdown to midnight was starting, and Elli and Aldo kissed as the clock struck twelve and the cheers went up in the room.

"Happy New Year, Elli, my beautiful one."

"Happy New Year, handsome." He kissed her again, long and

hard. They were breathless when they broke apart and Elli grinned at him. "Dang, that one kept going."

Aldo laughed and reached for her hand. "Ready to go down?"

"I must just use the bathroom to freshen up."

Aldo nodded. "It's just along this corridor, two lefts, and a right. I'll meet you back downstairs.

Elli walked along the hallways of the art gallery. There was no one around and her shoes clicked on the marble floor and echoed off the old stone. She found the bathroom where Aldo said it was and went in. She was washing her hands when she had the feeling of being watched again, that same feeling she'd had a while back in the alleyway. She whirled around, but the vast, luxurious bathroom was empty.

What is the matter with me, she started to think, when suddenly the door of the bathroom, partially ajar before, was yanked closed with a slam. Acting on instinct, Elli rushed outside and looked both ways down the hallways., For the briefest second, she saw the back of a tall man rounding the corner. He had dark brown messy curls, and Elli's heart began to beat heavily against her ribs.

Indio ...

She yanked the high heels from her feet and took off after him as fast as her lilac column dress would let her. She pushed through doors, glancing around the rooms, sure he had been watching her. She told herself over and over that it couldn't be him, and finally, breathless, she slowed and stopped.

This is ridiculous. It's just paranoia, she reprimanded herself.

Stop. Just stop.

He doesn't deserve your time, Moretti. He left you. He's gone, and there's a gorgeous, sexy man, with whom you've just had public sex, waiting for you downstairs.

She turned and retraced her steps back to the bathroom. Just as she was about to descend the stairs, a light breeze carried the scent of a man's expensive cologne to her. Indio's favorite. For a second, she breathed it in, eyes closed, then gritting her teeth, she stomped downstairs, almost angry now.

Aldo was chatting to Maceo and Ori as she returned to his side and slipped her hand into his. He smiled down at her and kissed her cheek, scanning her face for a brief second, leaving Elli feeling like he saw everything, even things she hadn't admitted to herself yet. Then he turned back to the couple, resting his arm securely around her waist. "Here she is."

"We were just saying, we should all have dinner sometime," Ori said to Elli, and Elli nodded.

"I would love that." Maceo, she noticed, didn't seem as enthusiastic as he had earlier and she wondered if she had done something to offend him. But when they said goodbye later in the evening, he kissed her cheek warmly.

"If you or your magazine ever need any artistic spaces or anything, please let me know. It would be great to work with you."

Elli smiled at him. "That sounds like a great idea. How about we talk around mid-January?"

"Great. Happy New Year." He handed her a card, and they said goodbye.

In the car on the way back to Elli's apartment, Elli leaned her head on Aldo's shoulder. "I'm glad we're staying in the city tonight."

"You don't like our house?"

She chuckled. "Your house, and of course I do. It's just my place is closer, and I'm feeling very, very horny right now."

Aldo laughed. "Well, that's just about the best news a man could hear."

She kissed his jawline as he drove to the parking garage

nearest to her apartment. Walking hand-in-hand back to her place, Elli looked up at him. "Aldo?"

"Yes, baby?"

"Feel like getting kinky tonight?"

Aldo grinned. "Always. What were you thinking?"

Elli hesitated. "I'd like to try the blindfold thing again. I think it would teach me to trust better."

He nodded. "We could do that. We could play some games."

In bed with her a short while later, he wound his tie around her eyes. "Can you see?"

"No," she grumbled. "And it's torture knowing you're naked and I can't see you."

Aldo laughed. "And you won't be able to touch me either. I'm going to tie your hands behind your back, beautiful."

"You are?"

"Yep. On your stomach, Moretti."

Elli laughed and obeyed, and Aldo bound her hands, tucking them into the small of her back as he rolled her onto her back again. Elli wriggled, smiling.

"You like that, huh?"

She laughed. "Surprisingly, yes. Now, tell me about this game."

"Well, you see this beautiful, soft belly of yours?" He ran a finger down her stomach, and she sighed happily. "Well, we're going to play a game of guess. I'm going to stroke various objects down it, and you have to guess what they are."

"Are all these objects attached to you?"

"Some of them will be." They were both laughing now, "Some I will have culled from your place."

Elli giggled. "And what is the purpose?"

"Apart from me spending quality time with your gorgeous abs? Well, here's the game. If you guess six or more right, you win, and I go down on you like I never have before. Get four or fewer, and you suck my dick and let me come into your sweet mouth."

"Dirty boy." But she was getting wet at the thought. "And if I get five correct?"

"Subtract one from seventy."

Elli laughed. "Oh, you are so on, Mr. Constanza."

She heard Aldo go back to the kitchen, then the living room. "I'm not trying to sway you, but you might want to look in my nightstand."

She heard him come back into the bedroom, the drawer of her nightstand opening. "Oh, ho ho," he said with a chuckle. "You've been holding out on me, you little minx." She heard the buzz of her vibrator, then jumped as Aldo touched it to her clit. "I have to say I'm relieved my only competition comes with batteries."

Elli smiled. She felt Aldo climb onto the bed, then his fingers stroking her belly. "Too easy. That's your hand."

"Did I say I had started? I was just preparing the playing field."

Elli started to giggle now, both with amusement and nervous anticipation. She felt him kiss her belly, then run his tongue around her navel.

"Okay, my beautiful Elli, what's this?"

She felt something cold, very cold, circle her navel. "Ice cube?"

"An easy one to start." He traced the ice around her belly, then to her nipples. Elli moaned at the sweet pain of the ice. Aldo chuckled softly, stroking it down her body and into her sex. Elli shifted, wriggling with pleasure, and when she felt Aldo's mouth on her nipple, cold from the ice cube, she gasped a little and arched her back to meet his lips. He teased her nipples with the ice cube until it melted, then kissed her mouth. "You taste like heaven, Elli. Next item."

A soft, ticklish thing, a feather, was next. Aldo traced it around her belly, then up and down her body as his other hand massaged her clit. Elli, enjoying the game and getting more aroused, guess the next three items as –well—a crystal ornament Vivienne had brought her from Paris, the edge of a wooden box from her desk, and the cold metal of her fountain pen.

Aldo kissed her. "You have five correct already, baby."

"We could just stop here and suck each other," she said, but Aldo laughed.

"No way ...this is too much fun. Next one."

Elli felt something cold and metallic touch her skin. At first thin, like a needle, and then flat against her skin ...like a knife? Elli's blood ran cold, and for a second she couldn't breathe.

"A knife?" she said hesitantly. She heard Aldo's sharp intake of breath.

"Of course not, Elli. What do you think I am? It was my watch."

"I'm sorry, Aldo. I wasn't accusing you of anything. Some people like knife play. I'm just not one of them."

"Me neither, Elli, especially after what happened to ..." his voice choked off and Elli felt terrible. She couldn't reach out to comfort him, her hands still bound behind her.

"God, Aldo, I'm sorry. I was insensitive. Please, let me up so I can hug you."

"No. It's okay. I understand why you would have guessed that. Let's just put it down as a wrong guess. Next one."

It was hard, but soft at the tip against her skin, almost silky. Elli, trying to cheer him up, smiling at him. "Is that your incredible cock?"

Aldo laughed and pushed her blindfold off. Elli blinked to see him tracing his cock around her navel. "Correct. Which means you win, beautiful. Now ..." He shifted down the bed and hooked her legs over his shoulders. "Hold on tight, little one." He grinned up at her, and Elli could see no lingering anger or hurt in his eyes. Aldo buried his face in her sex, and she sighed as she felt his tongue twist around her clit until it was hypersensitive, then he plunged his tongue deep into her cunt, almost violently, until she was screaming his name and begging him never to stop.

Afterward, they fucked until dawn and fell asleep together, lips almost touching, Aldo's big arm locked around her waist. To Elli's great relief, the nightmares didn't make another appearance, and when she woke in the morning, she felt rested and safe.

In the shower, she took him in her mouth and milked him until he was groaning and coming into her mouth. He lifted her afterward and took her against the shower wall, his big frame almost filling the tiny cubicle.

While Elli dressed, Aldo went out to buy fresh, soft rolls for their breakfast. He returned as she was brewing some fresh coffee. He held out a newspaper to her, and she took it, registering the anger on his face. "What is it?"

"Page eleven," he said shortly. She opened the paper and saw the picture of them leaving the art gallery the previous night. Aldo was kissing her. She looked up at him. "So, we've gone public."

"That's not the problem. Read the article."

Elli looked down and began to read. "What the fuck?" The article, far from just outing them as a couple, ripped into Elli's journalistic integrity over dating a subject of an interview and called into question whether it had been a legitimate article or a puff piece designed to sell her 'boyfriend's' business to the masses. There was no identification of the writer in the piece.

"Ms. Moretti seems preoccupied with Mr. Constanza's physical attributes far more than whether his philanthropy is genuine or masks a man whose ruthless business acumen means he leaves few survivors in his wake. But what strikes me most is this—since when has Il Mondo Italia been what amounts to a gossip magazine pandering to the elite? Since Ms. Moretti needed to get her rocks off, it seems. It is a sad downturn in the quality of a previously exemplary investigative magazine. Ms. Moretti, you should be ashamed."

Elli's hurt, and anger rose to the surface and she threw the paper on the table. "Fuck." She tried to keep the tears from welling in her eyes. She'd had bad reviews before. Of course she had—it was part of being a writer, but this was one step away from calling her a whore. She slumped into a chair and covered her face. Aldo stroked her arm.

"None of that is true. You know that, right?"

She nodded, but it didn't make her feel better. Being called a whore in public wasn't the way she wanted to start her New Year, but she knew that responding would only make it worse. Her cell phone rang and she saw it was Viv calling.

"I may be about to be fired," she said to Aldo, who shook his head. Elli answered the call. "Hey, Viv, guess you saw the article."

"Yes, I did." Vivienne sounded mad, "And when I get my hands on the writer of it, he'll wish he'd never been born."

"I'm sorry, Viv. I really am."

"You haven't done anything wrong, Elli. This article is completely unjustified, and what's more, false in every way. I can't believe the editor let it get through."

Elli sighed, somewhat relieved. "Look, I'm coming in to work. We can talk about it in greater depth and consider how we might respond."

"Are you sure? What about what the doctor said?" Vivienne asked.

"That was days ago. I'm fine. See you soon."

Elli put her phone back on the table. "Well, I guess the vacation is over."

Aldo leaned over and stroked her cheek. "Don't worry about this joker. Look, I'll walk you to work, but then I have to go away for a few days for work. Will you be okay?"

Elli was surprised. "You're going away?"

"Yes. Is it a problem?"

"You haven't mentioned it before is all. Where are you going?"

"New York. I'm sorry. I thought I had."

She shook her head. "But then again, there's no reason you should have to run anything past me, so don't worry about it."

"You sure, Bella? You look a little annoyed."

She shook her head, but the truth was, she was a little scared. This business trip seemed to come out of nowhere and she wondered if Aldo thought a little distance between them would be a good thing after the article.

Aldo was watching her, and as she got up, he pulled her onto his lap. "Whatever it is you're thinking right now isn't what's happening. It's just a short trip, and if I didn't know you had work, I would have invited you to come with me. "

Elli leaned into him, already missing him. "I know. I'm sorry."

AT WORK, after Aldo had kissed her goodbye and promised to heat her bed with his phone call later that night, Elli went to see Vivienne, who hugged her, then asked her to shut the door behind her and sit down. "I called the editor of this rag." She waved the offending newspaper in the air, still mad. "The article wasn't from one of his own people, rather an anonymous submission. He thought it made good points—which, by the way, it doesn't—and put it in. Elli, did you piss this guy off at all?"

Elli thought back, then shook her head. "I don't think so. But then that paper has never liked magazines like ours—we're too 'elite' or 'left wing.'"

Vivienne still looked unhappy. "Smearing one of my employees is not something I'm willing to let go, Els."

"Fair enough, but if we engage with them, it's like saying their opinion is worth something. I hate to say it, but let's just leave it alone. I'll just have to make sure that my future articles are ..."

"As good as they always have been," Vivienne said, a little forcefully. "Do not let this asshole make you feel as though you're not talented. You were born to do this, Elli, and you know it."

"Thanks." Elli got up. "I'm going to distract myself with some work. I'm fine," she emphasized, before Vivienne could check up on her yet again. "Sitting around at home won't do me any good."

As promised, she immersed herself in her work. It felt good to be back in her office, calling some of the shots in her life. She did some general research on some pending pieces, then called Maceo Bartoli and set up a meeting with him to discuss working together. "I'd love it if we worked on something that was both investigative and beautiful to look at," Elli told Maceo. "If we could do something actually in your own gallery—I've heard it's a beautiful space."

Maceo laughed a deep, sexy chuckle. "You should come have lunch with Ori and me sometime and have a good look around. Then you'll see it's chaotic and frenzied, but. yes, I adore it. We've managed to build it up over the last few years so that we have a family atmosphere. You would enjoy it."

Elli smiled down the phone. "I would love that." They set a date for the following week, and Elli said goodbye, feeling a lot happier. She also got a message from her colleagues, supporting her after reading the article. A couple of journalists from local T.V. reached out to her, but she politely turned down their requests for interviews. "I'm not the story," she told them, wishing she could go back to the relative obscurity she had known a few weeks ago.

It was three o'clock before she looked up from her work, and then it was only because she heard a commotion out in the reception area.

Suddenly, a girl with bright blue hair burst into her office. "Konnichiwa!"

Elli gaped at the girl. "Tandy? Oh my god!" She got up and the two women embraced, hugging each other tightly. Tandy, a part-Japanese, part-American woman in her early twenties had been Elli's best friend for a few years, ever since the younger woman started as an intern at the magazine. Tandy Li had only one ambition—to travel to every country in the world—and over the last two years, she had been doing exactly that, working her way (sometimes illegally) through the Americas and Canada, down to the Caribbean, and then to Europe.

Elli made some coffee and they sat in her office. Tandy told her she was in Italy for just a week. "I've finally got enough money to go to India," she said. "But I couldn't do Europe without coming back to say hi to my bestie. How're things? Viv said you're getting some decent sex at last."

Elli nearly choked on her coffee, but then laughed. "Nothing is sacred, is it?"

Tandy grinned. "Nope. You look good, Els, I have to say."

Elli smiled. "Well, I'm excited you're here, Tandy. Where are you staying?"

Tandy looked a little guilty, and Elli laughed, having

expected her to ask her to stay with her—it was an old habit. "You can stay as long as you want, Tee. You know that."

"The boyfriend won't mind?"

She hadn't really thought of Aldo that way before. Elli turned the label around in her mind for a moment, feeling oddly uncomfortable with it, before dismissing the feeling as yet another residue from the damn concussion. "The boyfriend is in New York for the next few days, so you're all set, as long as you don't mind sharing a bed with me."

"Have I ever?" Tandy rolled her eyes. "We're going to have so much fun. Listen, I have to go meet another friend, so can I come by your place around nine tonight?"

"Of course. I'll even go grocery shopping."

"Don't buy anything healthy."

Elli chuckled. "Oh, I won't."


ELLI LUGGED the grocery bags up the stairs to her apartment. Dumping her bags on the table and taking off her coat, she walked over to the small table beside the door to set her keys down—if she didn't, they'd be lost immediately. As she leaned down, she spotted a plain brown manila envelope just poking out from beneath the door. Frowning, Elli picked it up and turned it over. There was no name on it, nor was it addressed to anybody. Walking back into the kitchen, she set coffee brewing, then opened the envelope and shook out the contents.

A photograph slid out, face down, and when she flipped it over, she felt a cold fist in the stomach. It was a picture of her from about twenty minutes ago. She was emerging from a bakery several blocks away, looking sideways down the street, so she'd missed whoever it was who had the lens pointed her way.

What the fuck? She studied the envelope and photo minutely, but could not see any trace of a clue to who might have sent it. It was such an invasion of privacy—and so creepy. She remembered how she'd felt at the art gallery on New Year's Eve and that same prickling feeling chilled her skin. *If this is you, Indio Navaro, stop it. I've moved on.*

Maybe he had seen the picture of her and Aldo kissing. *Don't kid yourself, girl. Why would he care?*

Elli shook herself and stuffed the photograph and the envelope in the trash can. She unpacked the groceries and was wondering if she should cook something for a late supper with Tandy when her cell phone rang. Not looking at the Caller ID—she automatically assumed who it was, based on Aldo's earlier promise—she answered with a playful, "It's not quite bedtime yet. Missing me so soon?"

The caller whispered down the phone.

"You look beautiful tonight, Elli."

Her flesh crawled again and anger flashed through her. "Who is this? What the fuck do you want?"

A low chuckle, and she tried to pick out anything she could recognize in the voice.

"You, of course, Elli. Always you. It's always been you."

Elli gritted her teeth. "Well, asshole, you don't get to have me, do you? Who are you?"

"You know me, Elli Bella."

The shock was icy cold. "Indio?" her voice, a whisper, broke as she said his name.

He chuckled. "Who knows? All that is certain is one thing, beautiful Elli."

"What's that?"

"That soon you'll be bleeding out, whore."

And the line went dead. Elli dropped her phone and sank to the floor, trembling violently, unable to stop the panic attack, and that's where Tandy found her an hour later.

Tandy insisted on Elli reporting the call and the photograph to the police, but the terse officer taking her statement evidently thought she was a hysterical female, and soon Elli stomped out, followed by a furious Tandy.

"Motherfucker," she raved as she wrapped her arm around Elli's shoulders. Tandy had the height from her American father, almost six feet of her to Elli's five-five, and Elli was weirdly glad of it as they walked home through the dark streets. It was bitingly cold. Elli looked at Tandy a little sheepishly. "This isn't the homecoming I wanted you to have, Tandy. Maybe I'm making too much of this."

"A death threat? No way, Elli. This is scary stuff." Tandy sighed, shaking her head. "You know what's weird, though?"

"What?"

Tandy glanced at her. "Don't take this the wrong way, but I always was waiting for something like this to happen to you."

Elli was shocked. "Why?"

"Because look at you, Elli. You're so beautiful, so friendly, and yet when anyone gets close, they're banging up a brick wall. Someone was always going to get nasty, and I think this is it."

Elli was silent. "So it's my fault?"

"Hell, no." Tandy was vehement. "It's the fault of a civilization that leads men to believe they're entitled to any woman they want, and that murder is an option open to them if they don't get what they want."

"But I have let someone in," Elli insisted. "I hope you get to meet Aldo ...he's just the sweetest, sexiest guy. And he and I are growing closer every day ...in every way." Elli flushed, and Tandy grinned.

"Then he's probably not the one playing these games."

"Of course it's not Aldo," Elli said in surprise. "He would never do anything to hurt me."

"Of course, of course." Tandy waved her hand. "I was being

facetious. Elli, I know you won't want to go down this path, but ... do you think it might be Indio?"

Tandy knew everything about Indio and Elli's love for the man. Elli sighed.

"I would hate to think so. Besides, Indio knows that if he came back ..."

"You would dump Aldo in a second if Indio showed up."

Elli was stung. "I wouldn't."

"Hey, I'm not judging—but are you being honest with yourself?"

Elli could feel the tears coming again, and she looked away from her friend. It was a moot thought anyway—Indio was never coming back—so what did it matter if Tandy just might be right? "Please don't make this harder than it is," she said in a soft voice. Tandy hugged her.

"Sorry. Now, let's forget this nonsense and go eat our body weight in front of the television."

Tandy did a great job of distracting Elli for the evening, but when Tandy fell asleep on the couch just after midnight, Elli put a pillow underneath her head and blanket over her and went to her bedroom, realizing she'd never gotten the promised call from Aldo.

She grabbed her laptop and opened Skype, hoping he would be online. She had been debating with herself all night whether to tell him about the threats, but when she saw his smile as he logged on and greeted her, she demurred.

"Hey, gorgeous."

"Hi, Aldo. How's the Big Apple?"

"Lonely without you. I only got in a little while ago. Did you talk to Viv about the article?"

God, the article ...she hadn't thought about that at all since the threats. "It's all good. We're not going to respond to it."

Aldo looked a little surprised. "Wow."

"What?"

"Well, you were so fired up and now it seems like you've let it go."

Elli nodded, not quite meeting his eye. "Yeah, well."

"You okay?"

"Absolutely. Actually," she said, seeing Tandy stumble into the bedroom, bleary-eyed, and using it to change the subject, "I do have to tell you that I'm sharing my bed with someone else tonight." She grinned as Aldo's eyebrows shot up and Elli moved the laptop around to where Tandy was crawling into bed. "Say hello to Aldo. Aldo, this is Tandy, a good friend of mine. She's crashing here for a few nights on her way to India."

Aldo chuckled and said hello to Tandy, who greeted him, then promptly went back to sleep. Elli grinned at Aldo. "She showed up at the office today. No warning."

"Serendipitous," Aldo nodded, "I like you're not alone."

Elli gave a half-smile. "I'm a big girl now, Aldo. I don't need a babysitter."

"Sorry," he smiled ruefully, "I'm overprotective, I know. Scuzi."

"You're forgiven."

They chatted for a little longer, until Elli felt herself wilting and said goodbye. Aldo blew her a kiss, clearly seeing that their evening rendezvous was a no-go tonight.

"I love you, Elli. Sleep tight."

"Goodnight, Aldo. I miss you."

After she'd shut her laptop, she lay back. She felt guilty about not telling Aldo she loved him when it had been her mind lately that she might be falling for him. Certainly she was very,

very fond of the man, and she loved the sex—exciting and a little dangerous. Aldo being a billionaire didn't faze her—she had never been the gold-digging type. It was his money, not hers.

Elli closed her eyes and was asleep in minutes. She wasn't sure how long she slept before he nightmares came back, bloody and violent, and she woke, crying. Tandy inevitably was woken by Elli's panic attack and sat beside her friend as she gradually calmed down.

"It's still Indio, isn't it?" Tandy eventually said.

Elli sighed. "Less so. I think …I think I just need closure, you know? I have no idea where he is—even Googling him brings up his company, but nothing, and I mean nothing, about him personally. It's as if he's wiped himself off the face of the earth. Even gossip sites have nothing on him, and seeing he was married to that model, I'm surprised."

Tandy sighed. "Look, I wasn't going to tell you this …but I saw him. Now, because I never met him, I could have been wrong, but I don't think so. You can't replicate his kind of beauty. In Seattle. He was having dinner with a couple. This was about six months ago. He looked tired, worn down, and they were having a pretty intense conversation by the looks of things, as if he were upset and they were trying to help him."

Elli's heart was thumping with a sad heaviness. "He looked tired?"

Tandy nodded. "I didn't feel as if I could go over, so I thought it would be best if I didn't tell you. But he is out in the world, safe, if not happy. Does that help?"

Elli considered. "I don't know." She hesitated. "I keep thinking I see him, just a brief glimpse and then he's gone. Sometimes I think I'm going crazy. If it hadn't been for Aldo, I might have."

Tandy smiled. "You like Aldo, don't you?"

Elli smiled. "He says he loves me, but I haven't been able to say it back yet."

"Where is he at the moment?"

"Four Seasons in New York. He'll be back on Friday."

"Huh." Tandy was frowning.

"What?"

Tandy shook her head. "No, just something struck me. He's a solid-gold billionaire, right?"

Elli half smiled, half frowned at her friend. "So?"

"Well, it's just, if I had his money, I would be staying in the penthouse suite. From what I saw, that wasn't the penthouse of The Four Seasons."

Elli shrugged. "Maybe it was already booked. It was a last-minute trip."

"Yeah, maybe. Anyway, I'm getting off the topic. You've probably heard this a million times from Viv, Elli, but ..."

"Indio is history. Concentrate on the sexy man in your life now. Yeah, and I know you're both right. I am trying."

Tandy scooched down in the bed and tucked her arm around Elli. "Good. Now let's get some sleep, or you'll look like shit in the morning."

"So will you, bitch," Elli laughed.

"Not possible. Go to sleep."

WHEN HER FRIEND left for India on Thursday morning, Elli hugged her tightly. "Please come back soon. I miss you too much."

Tandy got a little choked, but hid it with her usual bravado. "Don't get all mushy. I'll be back before Christmas."

"Too long," Elli grumbled, but waved her goodbye at the gate and headed to the taxi stand.

She caught a cab back into the city and went straight to work. It was still early, six-thirty a.m., and the office was empty as Elli sat down and flicked on her computer. She filled the coffee pot as she waiting for her ancient laptop to boot up, then wondered if she should grab some pastries for breakfast. She patted her flat belly—she could do with gaining a couple of pounds, she thought. She had lost weight lately, mostly due to the Olympic sex she'd been having.

She decided to go down to the nearest bakery, a couple of streets away. Venice was just coming to life in the dark January morning, but there were few people around. The bakery was just opening, and Elli bought a couple of breakfast rolls and some pastries for her colleagues when they got into the office.

She was almost back, walking down the short street that led to the magazine's back entrance, when it happened. Suddenly, she felt someone slam into her from behind, knocking her flat against a stone wall. Elli cracked her head hard against the stone —the feeling was disturbingly familiar—but couldn't scream before her attacker knocked her to the ground and landed a vicious kick to her stomach. Elli tried to curl up in a ball, pain ripping through her, too shocked to cry out or fight back, but her attacker straddled her, his face obscured by a black mask, and reached into his pocket for a knife.

Oh, god, no ...

"Please, don't."

As he raised the blade to drive it into her, there was a shout. Elli heard footsteps running towards them. Her attacker took off, and Elli struggled into a sitting position on the ice-cold ground. Two young men helped her up, peering worriedly at her. "Are you okay, signorina?"

She nodded, shell-shocked, and touched her forehead, but there was no blood. Thank god.

"Tomas, you take her to the hospital while I get the polizzia," the taller of the two men said, starting down the street already.

Elli's hand shot out and grabbed him by the back of the sweater. "No!"

He stopped and both men looked at her, confused and concerned. "I'm fine," she assured them. "My office is right here. I'll go in and ... get help there."

With her rescuers staring unhappily after her, she walked slowly to her office and went in. It was still empty and she went to the little bathroom to clean her face of dirt. There was a small bump that she knew would bruise badly, but otherwise, aching stomach muscles apart, she was unhurt. But he had been about to kill her ...or had he? Something was bugging her about the whole attack—more than just the fact that her life had been threatened. The thing was ...it just didn't seem like whoever it was had his heart in it. Even though the men had interrupted them, he would still have had time to stick the blade into her and then run. So what the hell? Not to mention, why?

She poured herself some coffee and sat at her desk, opening her emails. Working methodically, gradually distracting herself from the earlier fear, she opened another message without looking at the sender and suddenly there were photographs of her, taken that morning as she walked to the bakery.

Elli stared at the shots, gritting her teeth as she scrolled through the extensive footage of her small excursion. But it was the last photograph that made her gasp. It wasn't a photograph of her; it was a beautiful, dark-haired woman in a pristine white wedding dress—pristine except for the blood spattered across it and the knife wounds in the bodice of the dress.

Yvetta.

"Oh my god." Elli was trembling. Suddenly it all became clearer to her. This wasn't about her or Indio—it was about Aldo. Someone was threatening to kill her to torture him. She grabbed her cell phone and called him, knowing it was after midnight in New York. She texted him, Aldo, baby, we have to talk. Please call me back when you can.

She'd barely hung up the phone when Aldo called her back, and after she quickly explained, his answer was definitive. "I'm coming back to you, Elliana. Do not even think to argue. No business trip is worth more than your safety. Umberto will pick you up from work and take you back to your apartment." His tone softened then, likely knowing she didn't respond well to orders. "Please, Elli, for me, pack your stuff. I want you safe in our home for as long as this psychopath is at large."

Elli hated the idea of being cooped up in an ivory tower, but she had to admit she was frightened. "Okay. Okay, Aldo, just until it's over."

Umberto, Aldo's sweet driver, gave her a grin as she walked outside the office to meet him. "Good afternoon, Miss Moretti."

"Call me Elli, won't you?" She got into the front with him, obviously something he wasn't used to. She grinned at him. "Umberto, I'm just a normal girl. Unless Aldo is with me, count on me riding up front with you."

She chatted with him as normally as she could, trying to distract herself from what was happening—circumstances forcing her to live with a man when she knew in her heart she wasn't ready.

She packed two suitcases, not wanting to have to keep coming back here, and Umberto took them down to the car for her. Elli looked around her apartment, wondering with sadness when she'd be back. She went to the window to look out over the Lagoon at twilight, seeing the lights of the city come on. A movement caught her eye below on the street and she froze. He was looking up at her, half hidden in shadow, and as she met his gaze, he moved back into the darkness and was gone. But she knew that gaze. It haunted her nightmares, and often, also her days.

Her heart thumping painfully against her ribs, Elli dashed down the stairs and out onto the street, ignoring Umberto's shocked face as she blitzed past him. Running down the alleyway to the street behind her home, she searched and searched, her hysteria bubbling higher and higher with each corner she turned without an answer. Finally, when it was clear there was no one to be found, she screamed out over the dark waters of the lagoon.

"Indio!" All her hurt, her rage, and her love was in that scream, and as she ran out of oxygen, she felt a hand on her back. Jumping away in sudden terror, she realized it was Umberto, looking at her with confused compassion. Leaning back into him, she began to sob as he guided her toward the car.

If you want to continue reading this story, you can get your copy from your favorite vendor by searching for the title:

**Dark Masquerade**

**(A Bad Boy Billionaire Romance)**

You can also find the e-book version by typing this link in your computer's browser:

https://www.hotandsteamyromance.com/products/dark-masquerade-a-bad-boy-billionaire-romance

## OTHER BOOKS BY THIS AUTHOR

**Saving Her Rescuer: A Billionaire & A Virgin Romance**

I was just trying to get away from my crazy ex for the weekend when I ended up in a giant pileup on the highway up to Gore Mountain.

https://geni.us/SavingHerRescuer

**Sensual Sounds: A Rockstar Ménage**

Lust. Lies. Double lives.

The rock and roll industry is full of people who are looking out for themselves and willing to do anything to rise to the top.

https://www.hotandsteamyromance.com/collections/frontpage/products/sensual-sounds-a-rockstar-menage

**On the Run: A Secret Baby Romance**

Murder. Lies. Fraud. Just another day in the lives of billionaires and women on the run.

https://www.hotandsteamyromance.com/collections/frontpage/products/on-the-run-a-secret-baby-romance

### The Dirty Doctor's Touch: A Billionaire Doctor Romance

I am a master. An elitist. I am at the top of my field, and I know what I am doing.

https://www.hotandsteamyromance.com/collections/frontpage/products/the-dirty-doctor-s-touch-a-billionaire-doctor-romance

∾

### The Hero She Needs: A Single Daddy Next Door Romance

He's the only man I've ever wanted...

https://www.hotandsteamyromance.com/collections/frontpage/products/the-hero-she-needs-a-single-daddy-next-door-romance

∾

You can find all of my books here:

Hot and Steamy Romance

https://www.hotandsteamyromance.com

# ABOUT THE AUTHOR

**About the Author:**

Mrs. Love writes about smart, sexy women and the hot alpha billionaires who love them. She has found her own happily ever after with her dream husband and adorable 6 and 2 year old kids.
Currently, Michelle is hard at work on the next book in the series, and trying to stay off the Internet.
"Thank you for supporting an indie author. Anything you can do, whether it be writing a review, or even simply telling a fellow reader that you enjoyed this. Thanks

Facebook
facebook.com/HotAndSteamyRomance

Instagram
instagram.com/michellesromance

©Copyright 2020 by Michelle Love - All rights Reserved
In no way is it legal to reproduce, duplicate, or transmit any part of this document in either electronic means or in printed format. Recording of this publication is strictly prohibited and any storage of this document is not allowed unless with written permission from the publisher. All rights are reserved. Respective authors own all copyrights not held by the publisher.

www.ingramcontent.com/pod-product-compliance
Lightning Source LLC
LaVergne TN
LVHW021658060526
838200LV00050B/2405